SAIL WITH ME

JEN TALTY

SAIL WITH ME
A With Me in Seattle Universe Novel
The Bowie Family Series
Darcie's Story
Book 2

USA Today Bestselling Author
JEN TALTY

SAIL WITH ME

A With Me in Seattle Universe Novel

The Bowie Family Series, Book 2

Jen Talty

Cover Design: Kari March Designs

Published by: Lady Boss Press, Inc.

fantastic, and the characters will keep you coming back for more. I can't wait to get my hands on future installments of the NYS Troopers series." *Long and Short Reviews*

"*In Two Weeks* hooks the reader from page one. This is a fast paced story where the development of the romance grabs you emotionally and the suspense keeps you sitting on the edge of your chair. Great characters, great writing, and a believable plot that can be a warning to all of us." *Desiree Holt, USA Today Bestseller*

"*Dark Water* delivers an engaging portrait of wounded hearts as the memorable characters take you on a healing journey of love. A mysterious death brings danger and intrigue into the drama, while sultry passions brew into a believable plot that melts the reader's heart. Jen Talty pens an entertaining romance that grips the heart as the colorful and dangerous story unfolds into a chilling ending." *Night Owl Reviews*

"This is not the typical love story, nor is it the typical mystery. The characters are well rounded and interesting." *You Gotta Read Reviews*

"*Murder in Paradise Bay* is a fast-paced romantic thriller with plenty of twists and turns to keep you guessing until the end. You won't want to miss this one..." *USA Today bestselling author Janice Maynard*

For the crew on Below Deck, thanks for the entertainment.

CHAPTER 1

*D*arcie Bowie curled her mic over her ear and tucked the white dress shirt of her uniform into her black slacks. She did a quick check of her hair and makeup in the tiny mirror that hung on the back side of her cabin door. She had to protect her hair from getting tangled up in the lines as they approached the dock, and she needed to make sure she still looked like a lady in hopes of getting the big tip.

A fine line she walked in her industry—one that she resented.

She squeezed the mic. "All deck crew, all deck crew. Prepare yacht for docking maneuvers. Man your stations." She secured her cabin—which should be called a closet and barely even that it was so tiny

—and hightailed it to the aft deck of the vessel. The end of a charter was never bittersweet.

It was always just fucking sweet.

Only, thanks to one very rich asshole she'd prefer never to lay eyes on again wanting a last-minute vacation, she only had one night off. That didn't make her happy. Not one bit.

"Darcie, can I make swing to port?" Captain Jim's voice crackled over the loudspeaker. Jim had been the reason she'd agreed to work on this yacht for the summer season.

Two big mistakes wrapped up in one massive dick. She should have known better.

She shivered.

Darcie held her fist in the air as she watched a group of young sailors in sunfishes learning the finer points of being out in the Sound. The first job she'd ever had was teaching sailing when she was sixteen, and it had been the best. To this day, she helped out in the marina, giving lessons and whatever else was needed during her downtime and whenever she came home to visit.

Of course, if she had a dollar for every time she'd been offered a job to manage the marina, she'd be able to retire.

"Ready to clear in five, four, three, two...ready to swing to port, Captain." This particular marina was pretty easy to navigate, especially considering they had secured the end of the pier for docking. Her crew could do it with their eyes closed.

For the most part, her team this season had been top-notch. They were a little immature, and she'd had to break them of a few bad habits, one of which her captain constantly perpetuated, but with only two charters left in the season, and the fact their relationship had ended, she had it under control.

She thought.

"Thanks, sweetheart," Captain Jim said.

Or not.

She rolled her eyes.

She hadn't liked being called that when she was his friend with benefits—in no way was she *ever* his girlfriend, not in the true sense of the word—so what made him think she'd like it now that they'd called it quits?

Fucking jerk.

As soon as the stern cleared the point, she dropped her hand. "One hundred meters from the dock," she said into the mic. "You are free to swing."

"Swinging to port," Jim said. "Prepare the bumpers."

"You're lined up perfect," she said. "Sixty meters stern to dock." She paced from port to starboard and back to port on the upper aft deck of the vessel. "You are clear five meters on each side." She waited until they were at the twenty-meter mark before giving the signal to toss the lines and secure the vessel. "Fifteen meters, Captain Jim."

"Taking docking engine to idle," Captain Jim said.

"Ten meters." She held her mic.

"Tapping reverse," Jim said.

"And we're tied off, Captain Jim."

"Perfect. Thank you, everyone. Let's get these guests off the boat. We've got one night to turn this bad girl around before our next charter. And just a reminder, I won't be staying aboard this evening."

Fuck. He had to remind the world that he would be getting laid. She should be happy he was no longer climbing on top of her. And she was, considering she'd planned on calling it quits at the end of the charter season anyway. But it still irked her how this entire fucking thing had played out.

"Deck crew, deck crew, this is Darcie. Meet me in the main salon for guest luggage disembarkment," she said over the radio, mentally slapping Jim across the face. Though she should be beating *herself* up. She knew his reputation. She'd seen it firsthand. Even suffered through being the shoulder a few of his conquests had cried on when he broke their hearts. If she should be upset with anyone, it should be herself because she'd known sleeping with Jim would only lead to being betrayed.

Again.

Not that it mattered. She'd only been looking for a distraction, and it wasn't as if she really cared for Jim.

She didn't.

Not in that way, at least.

Unfortunately, she still carried a torch for Reid, one of the primary charter guests coming on board tomorrow, and a man she'd spent the last year desperately trying to forget.

Craig, one of the deck crew, was the first to appear with two suitcases in his hand as he headed off the side deck. "What Captain Jim just did was a dick move, for the record." Craig set the bags on the cart and jogged back up the plank, passing his co-workers. "He shouldn't be rubbing it in like that." Of all the guys on her team, Craig had to be the most sensitive and empathetic. For the most part, it was a great quality, but Craig tended to take everyone's side and couldn't be trusted to have your back in general. He meant well, but he was going to take the side of whoever he was talking to in the moment.

Which meant he changed his mind all the time, and when confronted, raised palms to the heavens, saying that all he wanted to do was help.

"He's excited to see his latest notch in his bedpost," Darcie said. Of course, she could have had Jim fired, but that meant she would have been canned as well because she would have had to come forward for sleeping with her captain. Having his ability to lead the crew called into question because she'd gotten her feelings hurt was a pretty stupid thing to do.

Besides, she was better off without Slimy Jim and his shallow compliments filled with sweet nothings.

"Can't blame the guy for wanting to spend time with the love of his life," she said with a hint of sarcasm, disguised as dollop of support.

Craig handed her a couple more suitcases from the plank and gave her the evil stink eye, which looked more like a child trying to do a pirate imper-sonation, but it went horribly wrong. "Ever since he dumped you for Kim, you have made excuses for him. Why?"

"None of you even knew I was going out with him until the shit hit the fan, so why does it matter?"

"Because he's a dick."

"Well, we all have to work under him," she said.

"You could have quit," Craig said.

"Of course I could have, but I wouldn't give him the satisfaction. And oddly, I enjoy watching him squirm. And besides, since no one knows I had a thing with Jim, technically, I did nothing wrong."

Craig raised a brow.

"Okay. The bottom line is Captain Jim is much easier to get along with when he's happy, not when he's got a stick up his ass. That's why I'm defending him. So, let's go say goodbye to these guests, start this flip, and smile our asses off during the tip meeting."

"Are we allowed off boat tonight?" Bradley asked. "I'm asking for a friend. Not."

Darcie laughed. "We're rotating. But I'm asking that you don't get drunk. This is a short turnaround, and our new guests are going to be a pain in the ass. However, I worked it out so that you can at least have a meal in town, and I didn't want Haley to have to cook for you." Darcie adjusted her stripes as she made her way toward the receiving and unloading area.

"Once you have the outside hosed down and dried, you can go to dinner, but you have to be back aboard by 8:00 p.m. The interior will be going ashore for a few hours after that. For the record, I won't be staying on board tonight. I have family obligations, so Kirk will be in charge. Don't give him a hard time and make sure everything is done right. I don't want to get any flak from Captain Jim tomorrow. Got it?"

"Got it. But if I didn't know better," Craig said, "I'd think there was a threesome going on with you, the captain, and our former chief steward."

"Bite your fucking tongue, Craig," Darcie said. "If you must know, it's my parents' wedding anniversary, and we managed to get my brother home on leave. The whole family is here, and I had permission to leave the vessel before Captain Snake decided to stick his slithering, nasty body into that backstabbing bitch—"

"Why don't you tell us how you really feel about our ex-crewmember?" Kirk, another one of her team members, said as he loaded up the suitcases. He was the oldest on the team and the hardest-working deckhand she'd ever had.

He was also one of the most laid-back people she'd ever met. Not much got to Kirk. He didn't let the drama of the ship affect his work, and his mellow attitude was a breath of fresh air. She and Kirk saw eye to eye on many topics, and of all her crew, if she had to be stuck with anyone on a desert island, it would be Kirk.

"I wouldn't want to shock those poor sweet innocent ears of yours," she said, shooting him a sarcastic smile. Kirk had her back, and she trusted him. "I'm just glad she did the right thing and gave her resignation, because her life would have been hell if she stayed on this boat. I would have made sure of it."

"Even our chief stew would have turned on her eventually, and we know she's not your biggest fan," Craig said.

"Why do you say that?" Darcie shouldn't have asked the question, but she absolutely wanted to know, but only because Milia, the chief stew, was a stickler for the rules and sleeping with the captain was a big fat no-no, but Milia had been close to Kim. They spent a lot of time together and they rarely had any conflict.

"Because that's Milia's modus operanid, her MO. She always sides with the boson. Or the captain, because they are the highest rank on the ship. It would have been difficult for Milia, considering everything that went down, but in the end, she would have had to side with you because Kim quit. If she hadn't, she would have gotten fired."

"So would have Jim. And I just don't think Milia would have turned on Kim, ever. She has always sided with Jim on any issue when it came to me. But it doesn't matter anymore. Besides, there are only two charters left, so can we just forget all that shit."

"I'm down with that. Do we know how long this next charter is? I'm just asking because my mum is going to be flying in from Sydney, and I want to let her know what the best dates would be so I can actually pick her up at the airport. And how much time off do we have before the last charter?" Craig asked.

"This charter is three days and two nights, starting tomorrow at noon. Unfortunately, it cuts your vacation from four days to three," she said. "But Jim told me the owners of the vessel plan on making it worth our while."

"That sounds good, and if it's a good tip, all the better. I can use the money. Any idea who the primary guests are? It wasn't on the books when we left a week ago." Kirk ran a hand through his thick, wavy hair. She'd worked with Kirk on two other vessels. One out of Florida, and the other out of Greece. Both times, she was a deckhand and not a boson. Kirk hadn't liked working under her at first since he had more experience, and had applied for the job of boson, but he'd come around quickly and had become her second. She would hire him in a heartbeat.

If she were to continue in the yachting business.

Something she was seriously considering leaving behind altogether in a couple of years. She'd actually contemplated quitting when Jim humiliated her a few charters ago, when he decided it was okay to sleep with someone else, but then she would have had to explain her rash exodus to her parents, something she couldn't do—but only because her family would have a weird sense of pride if she failed.

She wouldn't give them the satisfaction.

Not to mention that no matter what happened, she wanted her captain's license, and she wouldn't stop until she had the chance to be at the helm.

She swallowed. While Craig knew nothing of the new charter guests, she knew a little too much. "Two business partners with four of their employees. They are celebrating some big milestone with their company." Reid's company developed safety products for exteme sporting enthuasists as well as similar products for companies that took people on excursioins such as white water rafting.

It was rare that anyone was injured, much less died during these excursions—but it happened. Which was why Reid was so passionate in his endeavor to make products that protected people.

Darcie had to wonder if Reid knew that she was a crewmember on the vessel he'd just chartered. If he did, she was shocked he had signed on the dotted line. The last time they'd seen each other had gone about as well as the last time she'd seen Captain Jim naked.

Pretty fucking horribly.

"Actually, you might have heard of their company," Darcie said. She couldn't remember if the television show that Reid and his partner had been on asking for investors had aired yet or not. She'd only seen the previews and had no intention of watching it. But if it had, Bradley, one of her deckhands and fellow sports enthusiast wannabee, would have seen it. He loved that show, and it was about all he'd talked about on the charter. That and what it was like to come eyeball to eyeball with a great white shark. "The Extremist Squad."

"Yeah. I know those dudes. They just got signed on to do some movie thing with some new technology they are developing. They are trying to get it approved for firefighter use. It has a bunch of tests it has to go through, but damn, that would be cool. And they are going to be on our boat, tomorrow?" Bradley snapped to attention as Captain Jim, along with the interior crew, made their way to the aft salon. The guests would only be a few paces away.

"Looks that way." Darcie rolled her eyes. "Why do you salute him?" she whispered. "It's so not necessary."

Bradley shrugged.

This last charter had been an easy one. Nothing bad had happened. No drama. Well, at least not with the guests. She couldn't say the same for her and the chief stew and the captain. Milia always had to take Jim's side on everything, and it made Darcie nuts. Of course, Milia had been Kim's best friend on the boat, so when Jim decided to sleep with the second stew while still in a relationship with the boson, things got really ugly, and it made sense that Milia would stick with her bestie.

However, it didn't help that Milia knew about Jim's extracurricular activities long before the rest of the world knew and decided to keep that piece of information to herself. Darcie also refused to acknowledge that she and Jim did their best to keep their relationship a secret. The only person who had any idea was Kim.

Oh. The irony.

She plastered a big smile on her face and shook hands with the guests as they went through the crew line like they would at a wedding reception. Right now, she hated her job and contemplated walking off the yacht when the guests did.

When she first started on this crazy career path, it had been exciting and wild. She traveled the globe, worked on various vessels, learned from some amazing captains, bosons, and other deck crew. She'd begun her career at sixteen, and her family thought she was nuts. Her father actually used the word *certifiable*. Her parents tried to bribe her into staying in college with a car and an apartment all paid for in full.

But stability wasn't what Darcie craved. Adventure and not knowing what would happen next is what she'd yearned for back in the day. Of course, having a boyfriend who liked to jump out of perfectly good airplanes just for shits and giggles didn't help tame the beast inside Darcie, and Reid Carson helped fuel her passions in ways she'd never dreamed. He'd filled her sails and her heart with a warmth she hadn't know she'd been missing.

And then he took it away, leaving her to drift in the middle of the open water all alone.

In the beginning of their relationship, he'd encouraged her to do whatever it took to captain her own ship one day. He'd told her there was nothing she couldn't do, and she'd believed him.

She still did.

Only, she'd lost faith in his ability to be a decent human being.

She let out a long breath. She was a week away from taking her captain's test.

Only asshole Jim could put an end to that if he wanted to; another reason she'd kiss his ass these last few seasons. If Jim didn't give her a glowing report, it wouldn't matter how great she did on the test, no one would hire her to captain their vessel.

At least not one that would bring on the kind of guests that would command a salary she could live off of, and one that would finally get her family to shut the fuck up about what a real job was all about.

The primary guest handed Captain Jim a thick envelope before turning and heading down the long pier with his friends.

"Let's meet in fifteen for our tip meeting, and then I will be off the boat until nine tomorrow morning." Jim smacked the wad of cash with his hand and double-timed it toward his cabin, waving over his right shoulder.

Don't look. Don't do it.

Darcie glanced toward the dock, and there stood Kim in a cute little strapless floral sundress and polarized clear shades. She smiled and gave a little waggle of her fingers as if they were old friends.

Which, they were.

Sort of.

She'd known Kim on and off for years. She'd actually recommended Kim for this crew when, about two weeks before the start of the season, they were still looking for someone to round out the interior, and Kim had just finished working on a vessel in Southern California. They weren't best friends, but they were colleagues and they got along well enough. And Kim had known how Darcie felt about Jim and her concerns about his wandering eye.

Well, it wandered right to Kim.

"She'd like to talk to you but says you won't respond to her texts." Milia stood by the stairs leading down to the main salon.

"I have nothing left to say to her."

"She has things she'd like you to hear." Milia fiddled with her ponytail.

"I've heard them all," Darcie said, taking a step to the right.

Milia followed. "You can't help who you fall in love with."

Oh for fuck's sake. Not this lame excuse for why his dick just happened to fall out of his pants and land inside her crotch.

"It's not like she wanted for this to happen. She actually tried to stop it. She asked him to back off more than once."

Darcie inhaled through her nose and let the breath out slowly through her mouth. She'd learned this little anger management trick from her sister-in-law. "Since you enjoy being in the middle of shit, why don't you go run down there and remind Kim that Jim, her boyfriend, the man she proclaims to love, was slipping between my sheets and hers for at least a good two weeks. And I'm sure Jim said he wasn't doing the nasty with me anymore, but I bet if we pulled out our calendars, we'd find some cross-over fucking going on." Darcie leaned in. "How do you think Kim is going to take that juicy little piece of information?"

"Why do you have to be so hurtful?"

"I don't want to be. That's the point. But if you keep this up, she's bound to figure out that Jim's lying about the fact he and I were still fooling around when he started doing it with your bestie."

"I don't know that to be true. You said so yourself you and Jim were on the way out."

Darcie really didn't want to hear another word of this utter bullshit.

"She just wants to clear the air. And not for noth-ing, the rest of us have to work with you. Maybe it would make it all a little easier if you had a sit-down with Kim and Jim. Like fucking adults," Milia said.

"Jesus. Kim and Jim. They sound like a damn candy bar or something," Darcie said, shaking her head. "No. I'm not doing a sit-down with the cute couple. You forget. Kim knew about me and Jim and she chose to sleep with him anyway. That's a pretty low thing to do."

"Darcie, Darcie, Captain Jim. Can you meet me in the bridge before our tip meeting?"

She tapped her earpiece. "On my way," she said.

"You can tell Kim I'll talk to her once I'm done with Jim. But just her. I'm not talking with the two of them, got it?" She'd lost her fucking mind. Shaking out her hands to try to calm her pulse, she made her way to the boat's cockpit. "You wanted to see me?" She set her radio down on the counter. She'd done her best to ignore Jim for the last month, and he'd done the same with her, but she had to admit the tension on the boat had become unbearable.

"I wanted to talk to you privately about two things. One personal and one about our next charter. Which do you want first?"

"You do like to shoot straight from the hip." She chuckled. "Let's get the personal shit out of the way."

He ran a hand through his hair and leaned back in the captain's chair. "I'd like to say I'm sorry. However, me apologizing for acting like a child at this point wouldn't do any of us any good."

"Oh my. Were you actually considering it?" She blinked a few hundred times and lowered her chin. She could handle working with Jim on a professional level, no problem. But being in the same space with him and shooting the shit?

That would just give her diarrhea of the mouth, which would lead her to saying something stupid, and that might piss him off enough to fire her.

"Why do you have to be like that?" he asked. "It's

not like you and I were having some great big love affair. We were just having some fun. That's what we both said."

"I agree, but you should have been a decent human being and—oh, why am I even bothering? Let's just put this crap aside. I know I can."

"But you haven't."

"Well, neither have you. Or do you want me to give you a laundry list of how you've treated me the last month since you and Kim became the king and queen of the Sound?"

"No. I'm perfectly aware. But I could do the same to you and this sarcastic attitude of yours has to be left on the dock. I feed off it, and it's just bad."

Darcie hated to admit that he was right, and she was going to have to find away to be less of a bitch around Jim. "I'll work on it. I promise."

"Good."

"Now, you mentioned you have some business stuff?"

"I'm not down with the personal shit." He shifed in his chair, adjusting his slacks. " I'm in uncharted waters when it comes to Kim and I'm a little flustered."

"I'm not even sure what any of that means. Or why I should care." She cleared her throat, doing her best to squelch the desire to voice the comments she really wanted to make.

He covered his face with his long fingers, bringing them together to a point at his chin. "I've always liked you."

"Jim, you're not making this don't-be-sarcastic concept easy for me. Can we get to the point, please?"

"When you told me that you scheduled your captain's license, I realized I wanted more out of my life. Only, it wasn't with you that I wanted it."

"Wow. Do you hear yourself? Why are you having this conversation with the woman you dumped for someone else?"

He had the audacity to smile. "I'm actually trying to thank you."

"For what?" Oh. Fuck. This should be good.

"I'm in love with Kim, and I've never felt that way before. Because of you, I was able to open myself up."

Oh for the love of all things fucking holy. She had to have her ex-boyfriend tell her that he was in love with the woman he was fucking when he was still dating her? And that it was all thanks to her? "Do you think I really fucking care, Jim?"

"Well, I'm going to ask her to marry me, and I didn't want you to hear it from anyone else. I wanted you to know that I was scared about everything and that I have no good excuse for the way I treated you—"

She covered his mouth with the palm of her hand. She'd heard all she needed to know, and she knew him well enough to know that he couldn't help himself. He was a shallow man who thought only of himself. "You're right. Nothing you can say or do will make up for what you did. Just don't go being an asshole to Kim. She deserves better."

"So did you."

Well, wasn't that a surprise wrapped in a pretzel? "I know," Darcie said, nearly choking.

"You and I need to be able to work this out through the rest of this season. I don't want us to be at each other's throats, or have you acting like this."

Oh, but he made it so damn easy. "So, let's get to work, okay?"

Jim scratched the back of his head. "You're really not going to like this." Jim leaned over, pulled open a drawer and handed her a piece of paper. He arched his brow. "When was the last time you spoke to Reid?"

"Reid Carson? My ex-boyfriend? Our next charter guest?"

"That would be the one." Jim gave her a sideways glance.

Yeah. She really needed to let the sarcasm sail away. "About eight months ago," she admitted. "I ran into him in New Orleans when I was there visiting a friend with my brother and a buddy of his, Matt Montgomery, who also happens to be a detective."

"And would your friend in New Orleans happen to be a cop, as well?"

"As a matter of fact, yes. Asher Smith. He used to work pretty closely with my brother. Why?"

"Actually, it doesn't matter, unless he can get a night permit for bungee jumping off Deception Pass here in Washington State and help me keep it quiet as hell." Jim leaned back and folded his arms across his chest.

"What other excursions do Reid and Preston want to do."

"I suggested a kayak trip through the rapids. That's no biggie and easily arranged, but this night bungee thing I can't get approved. At least not the way they want it."

She held all the rejections he'd gotten from the town and those responsible for such thrill-seeking adventures. "If you're thinking my brother can do something about this, I'd think again."

"I know. And if you ask him, and he can't make it happen, and our guests do it anyway…"

"Fuck," she mumbled. "I can't believe Reid would

put anyone in that kind of a position. He knows you'd lose your captain's license."

"I don't think he cares. He never liked me."

"Reid is a lot of things, but he wouldn't do that."

"Does he know you're the boson on this yacht?" Jim asked.

"I don't see how. He doesn't even know I'm living in Seattle," Darcie said. "When I told him I was buying a sailboat for a home, he thought I was joking."

"He doesn't know you very well, then," Jim said with a slight smile, though it turned serious quickly. "My communication has all been with Preston, Reid's partner. At one point, I wasn't even sure Reid would be on this charter. Anyway, Preston has made it clear the bungee jumping is happening whether or not it's sanctioned, and he also made a huge point of saying he doesn't want media coverage. This isn't a stunt to draw attention. This is a celebratory jump just for them."

"We can't let them do it," she said. "And in theory, it should be easy to stop them. But Preston doesn't take no for an answer easily."

"Preston will be at the docks shortly to confirm and give me an advance on a cash tip. If I say I can't deliver, he's going to charter with a different private company, and he says he's got someone in line."

"He's bluffing."

"I don't know. I heard chatter today that Gill's got a potential client."

"Gill's a dick and all talk," Darcie said. But Gill didn't boast, not unless he had something to back it up, which meant he was being used as a pawn to twist Jim's arm. Preston was good at manipulating any given situation to get what he wanted. He was a master at the game. A true artist.

But Reid? Not his style. Besides, she thought he'd given up all that adrenaline-junkie crap for the most part.

"What are you planning on doing?" she asked.

"I'm going to tell them it's all set, and then you and I need to figure it out because I'm not losing this charter, nor am I losing my license."

"You're seriously going to leave this all on my shoulders?"

"You are the boson. It is your job."

The next couple of days was bound to be the longest of her life.

She wasn't sure what would be worse.

Seeing Reid again.

Or seeing Reid right after she'd had her heart handed to her on a silver platter.

Although she had to admit she wasn't all that crushed about losing Jim. Her real issue had been the humiliation, not that Jim had dumped her. Because at the end of the day, she hadn't loved him.

"You do know we can't let them do it," she said.

"No. I don't know that because I've got the best boson in the business, and she's going to make it work. Got it?"

"Yes, sir." Motherfucker. Her ex-boyfriends were going to get her fired.

Or killed.

Or both.

CHAPTER 2

"**W**hy do you look so fucking miserable?"

Reid Carson set his phone screen-down on the table and glanced out over the docks. According to his research, Darcie's home—and sailboat—was docked in this marina, and if he wasn't mistaken, he could see the ass end of the vessel now. At least, if the information that she'd named it *Living the dream* had been correct.

She'd always said that if and when she bought a sailboat, that's exactly what she'd name it. And he certainly hoped all her dreams had come true. He couldn't think of anyone who deserved it more than Darcie.

He only wished he could have been part of her future. Not a night went by where she didn't enter his thoughts. She seeped into his unconscious, making his waking moments both amazing and torturous.

Reid lowered his shades, allowing what little sun was left to bombard his eyes. He stared at his business partner and glared. "Because you make me that way." He'd become sick and tired of pretending that things were getting back to normal between him and Preston.

Hell, things hadn't been right since Erin died. Maybe even before.

But the last few months had shown Ried how little he could trust Preston.

With anything.

"What the hell did I do now?" Preston waved at the waiter, holding up the nearly empty pitcher.

The waiter nodded, waving his index finger.

At this point, Reid didn't want to argue. If he could spend the next three days drunk, he would. But he had too many unanswered questions. "Do you really need to ask?" Fuck it. Getting drunk tonight would do him a world of good.

"Yes. I do," Preston said. "I don't get you, man. The two of us are finally back together, side by side, killing it, and you're acting like the roof just caved in."

Reid took his frosted mug and chugged the last of

his cold brew. There would be more alcohol, and then he'd stumble across the street and pass out until morning, where he'd start all over tomorrow. Maybe if he got wasted enough, he wouldn't be able to participate in anything Preston had planned on this stupid-ass vacation that celebrated nothing. "It's too soon. We don't have approval to go forward, and I don't know that my design is perfect. It hasn't been properly tested. Not even for the contract we just signed. I'm worried we're opening ourselves up for lawsuits."

"It's close enough. There is no need to do any more testing. The people at the studios are ready and excited. They've already used the suits twice and had no problems. You need to relax a little and let our lawyers take care of the legal shit."

A fucking night bungee jump from Deception Pass, while it would be exciting, was no place for him to relax, much less test out their new lightweight equipment. It was meant for highly trained professionals, not the masses anyway. It was all part of their Hollywood stuntman line, and none of it was ready to be manufactured.

Much less ready for any human to try it without proper safety protocols. And Reid knew that there was no way in hell that Preston or anyone on the team would want to put up a safety net. Preston hadn't learned anything from Erin's death. If anything, it'd made him feel more invincible.

A totally fucked-up concept if you asked Reid.

"We should be in research and development and talking with the fire department heads this week. Not hiring a private charter for a few days and acting like a bunch of frat boys."

"We worked hard for the movie contract. We deserve a little relaxation."

They had gotten the movie gig based on their personal experiences with extreme sports, both having competed in different events, as well as their desire for detailed safety.

Well, Reid's need for it. Which, according to Preston, had become an obsession that bordered on an addiction just as dangerous as not understanding that the seas could swallow you whole, leaving behind no evidence—and not a soul would ever find you again.

Maybe Preston was right. But Erin's death had changed Reid. And now, ten years later, he had to re-evaluate what was truly important, and he'd discovered some disturbing news.

He'd screwed up the last year something big.

Darcie Bowie, the one that got away.

He glanced toward the *Living the Dream* sailboat. The tall mast swayed in the gentle breeze. The lines clanked the metal, birds squawked as they flew over-head, and the water lapped at the sides of the boat, making a special kind of seaworthy music.

She'd accused him of using Erin as a personal emotional shield to keep people at arm's length, and Darcie had been tired of living in a dead person's shadow. Reid turned right around and informed Darcie that she had a chip on her shoulder the size of the great state of Texas and that she needed to stop trying to prove her worth to everyone, including her family—but especially the idiots in the yachting industry that thought women couldn't cut it.

That right there was half of Darcie's problem. She believed she had to fight for everything in her life. If there wasn't a battle, she didn't think she deserved it.

But the real breakdown in the relationship came when he told her that he couldn't live with her schedule anymore and if she wanted to continue to be with him, she needed to consider a different profession, knowing full well that she'd tell him to *walk the fucking plank.*

Her words.

Exactly.

For some godforsaken reason, since then, he'd always wanted to learn to sail.

The waiter returned with their fresh pitcher of brew and a tray of fried appetizers—Preston's favorites, because it was always about Preston.

"People are putting their lives in our hands," Reid said while the waiter set the food on the table. "We jumped the gun on this movie deal, and you know it. Hell, we shouldn't have even gone on that show." Thank God no one had invested.

"No. We didn't. And that is the wrong way to look at what we do." Preston took a good swig before wiping his face with a napkin. "People want to experience what thrill seekers do, only they can't do it the same way. We provide a minimal safety net."

"It's the minimal that concerns me." Reid wanted to bring up Erin, but he knew if he did, it could cause a scene, and he didn't want to fight with Preston. Not tonight. Reid had to remember that Preston had lost someone he loved, as well. He just handled Erin's death differently. Preston lived by the philosophy that people who took the kinds of risks they did, people who pushed limits and boundaries, often died young. And they died doing what they loved: experiencing life.

That's how he let the world believe he saw Erin, and while Reid had to accept there was a lot of truth to that statement, he also knew that Preston had many issues with his sister.

One of them was how she died.

Another was her growing vocal resentment for the industry and how unsafe it could be for both the guides and the guests. In any of the excursions she'd ever led during her traipses around the globe, she always ended up sacrificing her own well-being for those who simply wanted to step out of their comfort zone for five minutes.

Reid used to tell her all the time that she needed to make sure her safety equipment was top of the line. If it wasn't, she'd never be able to help anyone. And that was how she'd managed to make her death appear to be an accident.

At first.

But that lasted five minutes before everyone knew what she'd done.

Erin's need to put the safety of everyone else ahead of her own was her way to deflect attention. It made her appear to be something she wasn't. However, it wouldn't have mattered if Erin's equimpment had been faulty or not.

She wanted to die. No ifs ands or buts.

And Reid let Preston capalize on her death when they created their company. Reid did it to honor Erin and was damn proud of it.

But Preston? Well, Reid recently found out Preston only cared about making a name for himself and money.

And not necessarily in that order.

His sister's memory meant nothing.

"Look. I know you're concerned about the fire suits, and we need to run more tests before we can even bid them out to the fire departments. But they are good to go for stuntmen use. Can we at least agree on that?" Preston asked.

"I want your word you're not going to back out of taking this to the next level with the fire departments, and that you're not going to try to manufacture it in some sort of flame-retardant clothing line." Reid swallowed the nasty bile that had bubbled up to the back of his throat.

Preston's word wasn't worth shit.

Now all Reid had to do was gather more evidence to prove it.

"Scout's honor. Schedule the tests the fire marshals required." Preston knocked his knuckles on the table three times. "Now, can we have a little fun? You have to admit, signing that contract was almost as exciting as hitting weightlessness. I don't know about you, man, but I got a fucking hard-on."

At thirty-eight, Reid had lost his desire to conquer the world. His father used to ask when enough would be enough between finding the perfect adrenaline rush and the deal that made him the right amount of money.

His answer had always been that he'd know it when he hit it.

But he'd found out that enough would never come. There could never be total satisfaction unless you set an end goal, and most true extremists couldn't define what that final act would feel or look like.

And Preston had no idea what he craved other than a racing heart. The rush wasn't tied to finding his inner energy or living his best life. He had no clue what he really wanted, and he teetered on the edge, waiting for fate to push him over it.

Preston would never be able to find that perfect blend of danger, life, and death that set the heart to jumping after it came to a complete halt. Even if he did, he'd demand more.

Only what Preston failed to understand was that desire was actually death knocking at his door. That free-fall feeling he searched for was a mere illusion. It was like trying to take in that first five seconds of hitting Mach five and recreating it over and over again in a simulatious thrust of motion.

It was impossible.

However, Prestion would never quit, and Reid

would burn up upon reentry if he wasn't careful. Perhaps it was time to redirect Preston. Get him turned on to something a little more exciting. Something that would really get his blood pumping.

"Speaking of having a little fun... Maybe we can let the company run itself for a while. Ever since I came back to work, you've mentioned that you wanted to take some time off and do some hiking in Laos or Cambodia. You should absolutely do that," Reid said. "I'm doing well and can handle things here. I mean, you've been running everything while I was away, you might as well take a turn."

"Oh, trust me, man, I plan on it. But not for a few months. I do want to move on this partnership with the fire department. That's going to be huge because we can take it to so many other consumer products. So, between running the tests and tweaking the technology, a trip like that is going to have to wait." Preston raised a mozzarella stick and dunked it in some red sauce. "And I made a promise to my partner that I wouldn't rush."

Reid let out a slight chuckle, trying to fake finding this entire conversation amusing when in reality, his stomach churned. He wished he could trust Preston, but he'd lost all faith in him two weeks ago when he found out that Preston had taken a meeting with a manufacturer for the fire suits behind Reid's back.

Which meant, his partner was already planning on cutting corners.

And lying about it.

Reid should have known. This wasn't the first time Preston had pulled a stunt like this. Preston lived by the rule of asking for forgivness rather than permission.

Reid hadn't figured out how Preston thought he'd be able to push the deal through clothing companies before they'd even gotten the fire departments to vet the product, much less the federal government to appove the product, and not have Reid find out. It was something Reid couldn't even wrap his brain around.

Preston had done all sorts of things that made no sense since his sister died. For the first year after Erin's death, Reid had let a lot of things go when it came to Preston and his crazy stunts. He had to for his sanity. But as time went on, and he and Preston worked on their company, the divide between Preston and Reid regarding Erin's death grew larger. And three years ago, when Darcie came into Reid's life, Reid was all but ready to say goodbye to Preston. Reid had even begun working on an exit strategy, dividing up the company.

Fairly.

"I'm glad you've come around to seeing things my way," Reid said, but the words tasted bitter, and Reid didn't believe for one second that Preston would even consider doing things by the book.

"There are a lot of flame retardant and resistant materials on the market. What we're claiming—no, what I *know* our product can do—is save lives. We just have to make it wearable first and get the costs down for the fire departments. And then..." Preston waved his hand in the air. "We are not talking shop right now. And for the record, it's not that I've come around, it's that I'm not a fool, and I know you're right. That said, once we get to a certain part in the testing, it's full-court press and you know I'm not going to back down. You also know I'm right when it comes developing these products. We'll have to come out guns blazin', and you'll have to be ready for that." Preston made the clucking noise he always did when he was halfway to drunk and feeling a little cocky.

The arrogant part was a natural start for Preston.

He raised his hand and pointed his finger as if it were a gun and then dropped his thumb like he just pulled the trigger. "So, you can't be such an old lady, okay?"

Reid raised his drink. "To old bitches." *And to*

taking business partners down a notch, something Reid planned on doing.

"Holy shit. I don't believe it." Preston set his glass down on the table. The beer sloshed up over the sides. "You don't want to look now. But guess who just—?"

"Darcie," Reid whispered. He wiped his eyes as she stepped from the *Living the Dream*, her blond hair bouncing just at the tops of her shoulders. She wore a sleeveless white button-down blouse and a black skirt that stopped a few inches above her knees. Of course she didn't wear heels, she almost never did.

Hell, she barely wore shoes.

Darcie wasn't a thrill seeker, but she did like adventure that was for damn sure.

"I shouldn't be surprised to see her here. Seattle is her hometown." Reid stuffed a boneless chicken wing into his mouth. He coughed and pounded on his chest. He should have doused it in bleu cheese. A little too spicy for his tastes. He snagged his glass of water and chugged.

Why did he have to pick the table in the corner of the patio right next to the walkway that led to the docks? There was nowhere for him to hide. Even if he did manage to get up, she'd still see him as he'd have to navigate in her direction to get back inside the restaurant.

"Reid?" She paused, clutching her purse. "Preston?"

"Well, I'll be damned." Preston was on his feet in seconds, leaning over the railing and taking her hands in his, bringing them to his grimy lips.

Reid had half a mind to clock the bastard.

"Damned is one way to put it." Darcie smiled, though it had a bit of a sarcastic flare to it by the way the corners curled. She'd never cared for Preston, and the feeling had been mutual. "How are you?"

"Doing great," Preston said. "You look magnificent. As a matter of fact, I'd say you're glowing. Isn't she glowing?"

Reid stood and held out both arms, ignoring Preston and his obnoxious compliment that was meant to be a dig more than anything else.

Thankfully, she didn't deny Reid a brief hug. It ended long before he was ready to let go. Her skin heated his body like a fleece blanket in the cool Seattle night air. When he'd first met her, she'd stolen his breath and stopped his heart. She'd filled the emptiness in his soul, and at the same time, reminded him that most people either disappointed him or left him with a broken heart.

She'd done both. But the difference had been that he'd forced her hand.

"You do look good," he whispered.

"So do you." She tucked her hair behind her ears, something she always did when she was nervous— which honestly wasn't very often. "I heard you were in town."

"Where did you hear that?" Reid held her hand, running his thumb in a small circle over her soft skin. Every night before he closed his eyes, he brought up a memory of Darcie. He held onto it until he drifted off to sleep, and when he woke in the morning, it was as if she'd been right there with him all night.

He once tried talking to a therapist about why he held onto Darcie harder than he'd held onto Erin, as if he hadn't loved Erin enough.

The shrink had told him that his heart and mind knew that Erin was gone, and Darcie was only a phone call away.

Reid stopped seeing that psychologist and never called another one.

"I'm the boson on *The Weatherby*, the vessel you've chartered for the next three days."

"No way. I didn't know that, or I might have had second thoughts. No offense," Preston said. "And not because I have any problem with you. However, the last time the two of you were in the same space, it ended with my boy here looking like someone used him as a punching bag."

Darcie flicked her hair over her shoulder. "Someone kind of did." She let out a slight laugh. "Sorry. I couldn't resist."

"No worries," Reid said. God, he missed that sweet noise that cut through the rest of the evening chatter like a motorboat gliding across the calm Sound on a quiet night.

"That was a while ago, and I think we're both past it," she said.

"I agree." Though he wasn't past being in love with Darcie, and the way his pulse raced out of control was proof of that fact. "Where are you headed? Maybe you could have a drink with me."

"You mean us," Preston interjected.

"No. I mean me," Reid said.

"Thanks for the invite, but it's my parents' wedding anniversary, so I'm off to their house for a big party. My brother Troy was able to make it in, so I best make an appearance or I'll never hear the end of it."

"How are all your siblings?" Reid asked. After Erin died, he'd vowed that he'd never get tangled up in anyone's family again.

Until Darcie sailed into his life and turned everything upside down.

"Jagar got married, and his wife is pregnant."

"Holy shit. Well good for him," Reid said. "He's a good man."

"He's the best," Darcie said. "Since I've got the two of you together, I want to talk to you about Deception Pass."

"We can talk about that tomorrow," Preston said.

"My captain said it was an important part and that the charter hinged on the activity. And, well, it's not going to be easy. So, I need to know where we stand."

"You always were a straight shooter," Preston said. "I can respect that. I am, too. And, just understand we're going to do it no matter what. So, it really doesn't concern you."

"But it does, Preston. And you know it. I can't turn my back and pretend I don't know."

"Actually, you can." Preston was always one to skirt the rules. He was the complete opposite of his sister, and sometimes Reid wondered if Preston pushed the limits to see if that great big hole that'd swallowed his sister would swallow him, too. "You know we won't take unnecessary risks."

"We understand the conditions have to be right," Reid said, knowing he needed to defuse the situation. He would have to continue playing the equalizer between these two because Preston wouldn't back down.

And Darcie would push his buttons.

But really, the jump wasn't a big deal.

Reid understood it had more to do with the number of suicides the bridge had each year and the fact that a thrill-seeking company ran bungee jumps regularly at a bridge nearby, one at a safer location. "If the wind is too strong or anything is out of place, we'll call off the jump."

"So, no matter what, you're with Preston on this?" she asked with an arched brow.

"I'd rather we have the proper permits, but yes. I'm all in." Reid didn't want to take Preston's side. As a matter of fact, he wanted to tell the man to fuck off, but Reid was walking a fine line, and he couldn't show his hand.

Not yet anyway.

Preston puffed out his chest. "I'm sure you can figure this out for us."

"You're putting me and my vessel between a rock and a hard place if we can't get the paperwork," she said.

"Then let's get what we need in order to make all of us happy," Preston said. "I'm sure you and your captain can work some kind of magic for us."

"It might not be possible. And you boys have to accept that," she said. "Sorry. I've got to run."

"Please, tell your family I said hello, and congratulations to your parents," Reid said.

"Will do. I'll see you boys tomorrow." She squeezed Reid's hand and smiled before continuing down the dock toward the parking lot, her hips swaying in that perfect motion that made him want to go run after her and beg her to meet him for a drink.

Reid inwardly groaned. Seeing her again served as a doubled-edged sword.

"Did you know she'd be on that boat?" He sat back down and glared at his business partner, wondering why the fuck they were still working together. They didn't even like each other much anymore, though they pretended well enough, they could be up for an Academy Award.

"You've got to be fucking kidding me. If I'd known, I would have blown up the damn ship. If you'd like to cancel, I will."

"No. I don't want to bail." He waved his finger. "And you're not going to give her a hard time. You're going to have a fabulous fucking time and let her do her job. I won't tolerate conflicts. Not if you want me totally on board with moving forward with the contracts with the movie companies and potentially persuing manufacturing." Reid held up his hand and swallowed the vomit that trickled up to his throat as he lied through his pearly white teeth. "If all the rigorous tests I set up go well. Though that could take months."

"Fine on the tests." Preston let out a short breath as if conceding under protest. "And just to be clear, I can behave. Really, I can. The question is, can you keep your dick in your pants?"

That was a fair question when it came to Darcie, but he had it on good authority that she would *rather have all the pubic hair on her body plucked one follicle at a time than ever hook up with him again.* He was pretty sure she'd shut him down if he made a pass. And did he want to open that can of worms again?

They'd still have the same problems they had when they broke up a year ago.

His business decisions were still driven by his dead ex-girlfriend, and the woman he currently loved wouldn't consider a job that had her in one state for more than three months out of any given year. It was the same rock and hard place, and it was still as uncomfortable as fuck, the same as it was a year ago.

They wanted different things, and he still had one foot in the past.

CHAPTER 3

*D*arcie entered her childhood home from the back patio and made her way into the kitchen, where she poured herself an extra-large glass of expensive red wine and took three hardy gulps. Her family was used to her being fashionably late. It was her role, and she didn't want to disappoint them.

And she was still shaken up by seeing Reid.

Sexy as all get out with his low-hanging jeans, black V-neck shirt tucked in, and a dark belt with a sexy cowboy buckle. His hair with its thick dark wave that curled across the back of his neck and perfect highlights made every girl in the room want to run their fingers through it and ask about his conditioner and any other products he might use.

The kitchen door screeched as she made her way

down the Bowie hallway of fame and into the great room. Ten years ago, she'd tried talking her parents into making the kitchen open to the rest of the house, but they liked the old-fashioned separation. And right about now, as she took another sip of liquid of courage, so did she.

Pressing her back against the wall, she closed her eyes and took in a long slow breath, focusing on the deep timbre of her father's voice.

"I love these little cookies, Nic. Your bakery is the best," her father said. "I just wish I could drive by once in a while and not stop, but it's impossible. It's like my car has your address on autopilot or something."

"My Nic. She does make the best decadent treats within a hundred-mile radius. Or more," Matt Montgomery, Nic's husband, said.

Darcie's mouth watered at a vision of her and Reid sharing a piece of chocolate cake the weekend she'd brought him home to meet her family. She'd thought he was the one.

The one who understood her and accepted her for who she was, not what he wanted her to be.

But that had all ended when he made it clear that her going for her captain's license was something he would support, but not something he could get on board with long-term. If they were to make a go of it in a forever kind of way, she needed to find a new career path.

"Save some for Darcie," her mother chimed in. "I got those little chocolate ones with the vanilla frosting specifically for her. They are her favorites."

"No way," her father said. "If she can't show up on time, then too bad for her. Besides, that job is taking her nowhere and fast. Did you know that Hector offered her a job managing the marina and running the sailing school? And she turned it down. I can't believe she'd do that. That girl needs some stability in her life. She's always running off into the sunset, chasing some pipe dream. Only she doesn't even know what the hell she wants."

"She called and said her boss threw her a curveball and she's got a charter in the morning so she's got to flip the boat," Jagar, her oldest brother, said. "And she's taking her captain's license test soon. She loves what she does, and it's not like my or Troy's jobs are conventional. I mean, I've been shot. Twice."

"Don't go getting your mother all riled up about that now," their father said.

At least Jagar tried to stick up for her most of the time, though he did agree that her job was a bit harsh and that, at some point, she should consider a change.

"For as long as I've known Darci," Nic said, "she's

wanted only one thing, and that's to be on the water. She'll figure out what that looks like soon enough. She's still young."

"But she's not getting any younger," her father said. "Yachting isn't a stable profession. Too many unknowns. Too much risk."

"I really don't understand her industry or how it works. And why the hell is she living on a boat?" her other brother, Troy, said. "I mean, really, who lives on a boat?"

"You're a sailor. Don't you live on a dinghy that floats sometimes?" Ziggy asked.

"That's different. And I don't think you can call a nuclear-powered aircraft carrier a dinghy. Besides, isn't our baby sister living on like a fifty-foot sailboat? Is that like a Tiny House thing?"

"Not sure it matters where she lives since she's never home," her father said. "And it's worse since she and Reid broke up. I really thought he was the one. I don't know what she's so afraid of. As soon as she gets close to someone and things are going good, she runs. And now she's not giving herself any breaks between ships. She goes right from one charter season to the next. We're just lucky she got a job here for the summer."

"I wonder what Reid is up to these days," her mother said. "He was a nice young man."

"I miss that boy," her father said. "Best thing that ever happened to Darcie, and she just tossed him away. Much like she did college and that opportunity she had at that sales job."

Her mother laughed. "You thought Reid was too old and wild for her when she started dating him."

"He had Jagar run a background check," Matt said.

"I changed my mind. He was perfect for her, and if I had his number, I'd call him and tell him," her father said.

Fuck. Her father would reach out to Reid because her dad, God love the man, was a meddler. Worse than her mother.

"We don't know what went on behind closed doors," Ziggy said. "And let's not forget they broke up in part because he demanded she give up something important to her. That's a pretty uncool thing to expect of someone."

Darcie pinched the bridge of her nose. While she wasn't going to go chasing after Reid—that ship had sailed—she *was* contemplating her career choice in a long-term sense. She was tired of the traveling. Tired of the drama. Tired of dealing with childish deckhands who only wanted to get wasted and laid when they were off duty.

Simply put, she was just plain fucking tired, and

she didn't have it in her to live the life of a yachtie anymore. She could get a job as captain of one of the ferries. She'd be on the water doing what she loved.

It was an option.

She groaned. Okay. Perhaps not. She'd rather teach sailing. And, truth be told, she still wanted to captain a superyacht for maybe a year—or two.

But then she was done.

Her family had a point, and perhaps it was time she listened.

About her career.

Not Reid.

It was also time to shut them up. They'd had their gossip fun.

She inhaled sharply and let the breath out slowly as she plastered a smile on her face and entered the family room. "Hello, family. Sorry I'm late. Hope you enjoyed talking about me."

"It wouldn't be a family gathering if you didn't show up last," her sister Ziggy said with a big kiss and hug. "And if you mention the fact that I'm dateless, I will scratch your eyes out," she whispered.

"Ziggy. What? No date? Again?" Darcie did a little curtsey.

"I'll get you for that," Ziggy said, holding up the plate of cookies. "I think these are all for me."

"Not." Laughing, Darcie stretched out her arm and snagged a couple of the cookies.

"You know, I brought another box." Nic waved her hand toward the kitchen.

"I think we better go get them." Matt took his wife by the hand and led her through the maze of family and close personal friends.

"Look at you." Darcie took her sister-in-law, Callie, by the hands. "You actually look pregnant."

"Better than looking fat," Callie said.

Darcie kissed her brother Jagar. "Are you ready to be a dad?"

"Nope," he said, looping his arm over his bride. "But I don't have a choice anymore, now do I?"

"I guess not." Darcie laughed. "I will enjoy watching you attempt this." She patted Callie's belly. "You do know my big brother dropped me on my head when I was a baby."

"Everyone dropped you," her mother said.

"Right. That's your excuse for why I turned out this way."

"Those are your words. Not mine." Her mother held out her arms and wiggled her fingers.

No matter what, Darcie would always be the baby of the family, and there was nothing she could do about it. She just wished everyone would stop treating her like she was incapable of making grown-up decisions.

"Hey, Mom. Dad. Happy Anniversary." No matter how the family dynamics played out, or the razzing she took, she would always click her heels together and remind herself that when push came to shove, these were her people. Whenever the world caught her off guard, her parents and siblings had her back.

No matter what.

Even when they disagreed with her and her life choices.

There was still no place like home.

"How's my pumpkin?" Her father kissed her temple and hugged her close. "I hear you have to leave bright and early in the morning."

"I hate to do this, but I won't be staying the night. I've got to sleep on the charter tonight." Total lie, and she wasn't going to sleep on *The Weatherby*. Nope. She was going to get a bottle of tequila and do a few shots before climbing into her bunk to pass out, and hopefully not dream about Reid.

"Do you have to?" Her mother lowered her chin and fluttered her lashes over those big blue eyes.

"Ma. That only works on Dad." Troy laughed. "But I've got some bad news, too."

"No." Her mother raised her hand and cupped

Troy's cheek and gave it a good shake. "You have to leave tonight, too?"

Troy nodded. "Unfortunately. I have to be on a C-150 transport plane leaving for Germany at one in the morning. I'm lucky that I got to come at all. Duty calls. You know the drill."

"We're just glad you got to be here, son." Her father clapped Troy on his shoulder. "We understand and we appreciate what you do for our great nation."

Darcie resisted rolling her eyes. Both her brothers got a shit ton of respect, and they deserved it. One being a fighter pilot for the Navy, and the other being the Chief of Police for the Langley Police Department. They were noble professions, and she was honestly insanely proud of her older siblings. They inspired her every day to be a better person.

And her sister, Ziggy? Wow. She was a firecracker who didn't take no for an answer and always got what she wanted. Darcie had always wanted to be more like her sister, but Ziggy had this big personality and always managed to be in the right place at the right time.

But Ziggy didn't work in a man's world, nor was she constantly looked at as if she didn't cut the mustard.

It wasn't that Darcie worried she wasn't good

enough. She knew she was good at her job and that she'd make a great captain. She had the skill set, the passion, and she knew more than half the yahoos who went into yachting in the frist place. But she struggled because most of her efforts ended up washed out to sea because yachting was still a man's world, and no one would take her seriously. And even if they did, she still felt like she had to prove herself to the point where it became a ridiculous game.

"We're so blessed to have such great kids and soon to be our first grandbaby." Her mother planted her hands right on Callie's stomach. "I can't wait to meet this little creature. And more importantly, I so look forward to watching Jagar try to change a diaper."

"You and me both," Callie said. "I bought a toy baby for him to practice on."

"Yeah. That's not happening," Jagar said. "I'll have you all know I plan on being the best dad ever."

Darcie laughed. "I'm struggling with that concept."

"Isn't everyone?" her father said.

Life in the Bowie household had been filled with laughter, love, and a shit ton of teasing. No. More like harassing. Darcie had learned at a very young age that if she were going to survive in this family, she had to balance dishing it out and finding solace in her favorite hiding places when the energy level was at a category five.

She loved her family and wouldn't give up the razzing for anything. She just wished she knew what to do with her life when her yachting journey came to an end. Being on the water had been all she ever dreamed about, but she didn't want to be in the Navy. That wasn't the right career. The military wouldn't give her the proximity to the sea she craved. She could have ended up in a land-locked post, doing a job that had nothing to do with the water. She'd considered being a marine biologist for about five minutes in high school, but college wasn't her cup of tea either.

Sitting still was something she hadn't ever mastered.

"Thanks for the vote of confidence, people." Jagar lifted his wine and took a long sip.

"Awe, don't worry, babe. I know you'll be a good daddy." Callie patted Jagar's chest.

"I'm glad at least one person believes in me," Jagar said.

"Only because you made the decision to marry me." Callie smiled brightly. "Otherwise, you'd be doomed."

Darcie's heart swelled. She could give her family

shit all day long about their judgments, but they loved her and only wanted her to be happy. She knew that without a doubt.

All she had to do was figure out what happy looked and felt like. She knew from her older siblings that it sometimes took a while for the roadmap to show the actual directions. Wow. Her thoughts told her that perhaps the wine had gone right to her head. Good call on her part by using Lyft this evening.

"I don't know, Callie. He couldn't take care of me when I was a kid to save his sorry ass. He once left me on the ferry. I rode it back and forth five times before anyone found me," Darcie said.

Jagar waved his finger. "I didn't lose you or leave you. The truth is, you ditched me, and I totally freaked out. You didn't want to get off that damned boat, and you hid from me. I ended up having to call the cops. We both got in trouble that day."

Darcie laughed. "That has to go down as one of my fondest memories of childhood." She plucked a mini egg salad sandwich off one of the trays. She stuffed the entire thing into her mouth and prepared for the onslaught of flavors. Her mother always stuffed a cucumber in the center, and to this day, it surprised her tastebuds. "Jagar, can I talk to you for a moment?"

"Sure. I need to freshen up my drink. Anyone else want something from the kitchen?" Jagar asked.

"I'll take a water," his wife said.

Jagar looped his arm over Darcie's shoulder as they meandered down the long hallway where every accomplishment that any of the Bowie children ever achieved hung proudly.

Including her waving goodbye the day she left for her first yachting adventure.

She sighed. "Why does Dad have to belittle everything I do, and yet he does...this." She tapped the picture.

"You could have done exactly what he wanted you to, and he'd still give you shit for it. It's just the way he is."

"Well, it's annoying, and I wish he would razz you guys half as much as he does me."

"You forget—or you were too young to remember—but we've all had our fair share of Mom's and Dad's judgments," Jagar said. "I'm glad you got me alone. I actually have something I need to tell you, and you might need to sit down for this."

"Nothing can shock me today." Darcie found the bottle of red wine and topped off her glass.

Her brother did a double-take. "Maybe you already know that Reid's in town."

"I just ran into him. But worse, his company is my next charter."

"That fucking sucks." Jagar stuck his head in the fridge and pulled out his favorite beer. He twisted off the cap and tapped the longneck against her glass. "I still don't understand why you broke up." Jagar held up his hand. "Yeah, yeah, yeah. I get it. I meant it as a rhetorical question. I don't need you to give me all the reasons why you and Mr. Perfect didn't work out."

"Obviously, he wasn't so spectacular." When she and Reid called it quits, it had been Jagar's shoulder she cried on the most. He'd understood what it was like to lose the one person who understood you better than you did yourself.

Only Callie came back in his life, and now they were married and having a baby. Jagar got lucky and got a second chance at love. "How did you know he was in Seattle?"

"There was some chatter about him and his buddies doing a night bungee jump off Deception Pass. That kind of stuff always ends up as gossip in my office."

"They couldn't get approval for the jump. Which honestly, I don't understand. They are professional extremists. It's not like they don't know what they are doing."

"We had three jumpers this year alone. In general, we're afraid it will make it more enticing for suicide jumps off Deception Pass, and that's something we don't want."

She hadn't thought about it in those terms. It made sense. "They could get approval for another night jump on another bridge?"

"Probably. Maybe. I really don't know. It's not my area, but I could do some checking for you."

"That would be awesome. I know I can talk Reid into an alternative jump. Preston, on the other hand... He's an entirely different story."

"It's just a bungee jump. It's not that thrilling, considering what those two have done in their lifetimes. What else do they have planned on their little vacation?"

"Kayaking the rapids. Outside of that, just the toys we have on the boat. To be honest, Preston is going to be bored as shit, but Reid will be fine. He does know how to relax."

Jagar took another swig of his beer. "How was it to see him again?"

"Weird. Awkward. Normal. Nothing out of the ordinary. It's hard to explain." She leaned against the counter and folded her arms around her middle. "He looks good. Too good."

"Did you expect him to have gained fifty pounds, stop shaving, and quit using deodorant?"

"Considering the last time I saw him, that wouldn't be such a stretch."

"You went on with your life too, so you can't begrudge him for moving on with his."

She hated it when her brother made sense, and her mind had the audacity to agree with the level-headed thinking as if she had no right to throw a temper tantrum and act all indignant. "You could break out the baby violin and have a pity party with me. I mean, I ran into him right before I got here and had to listen to everyone talk about my career and ask when I was going to get a real one. Not to mention, they like my ex-boyfriend more than they like me."

Jagar laughed. "Reid did fit right in unlike that James asshole. How is Captain Jim?"

"He's getting engaged and laid tonight."

Jagar choked on his beer. "Engaged? That's quick."

"Well, I didn't call him quick-draw Jim for nothing."

"Jesus, Darcie. I never needed to hear that come out of my baby sister's mouth."

She waggled her finger. "I could start talking about the first time I had sex."

"Please don't. I still can't look at Tim and not want to punch him in the face."

Darcie smiled. Life didn't get much better than hanging with her family. "Will you please help me get permission for Reid and his team to jump from Deception Pass or find me a bridge of similar height and danger level that I can get them to by water?"

"Sure thing," Jagar said. "You should ask Matt, too. He knows more people in higher positions than I do. But Asher might be the best bet."

"But he's in New Orleans now."

"He was well-liked in the department and is connected as hell. If anyone can make it happen, he can."

"You take care of Matt, but don't do it tonight. I don't want to bug him at our parents' party or around family. I especially don't want Dad to know Reid is in town. I'll get ahold of Asher." Darcie used to babysit for Asher's daughter. She'd seen Asher through some dark days, and Asher always told her that if she needed anything at all, just to give him a call.

Day or night.

She glanced at the digital clock displaying the time in red. Eight-thirty. It was even earlier in New Orleans. She'd be reaching out to Asher tonight.

"Actually, wait on pushing Matt until I've heard back from Asher."

"Why?" Jagar asked.

"Let's see what Asher says first. I know Reid won't want this to be a spectacle, and Preston made it pretty clear that he didn't want any hype. They just want a team jump. The more people we get involved, the more the masses might find out. Do you really want a ton of people out by Deception Pass, at night, hoping someone dies?"

"You've got a good point there, baby sister. Let me know what Asher says and who he talked to so we're not doing double duty."

"Thanks." Now all Darcie had to do was get through the charter without throwing herself at Reid and begging him to sleep with her for old times' sake.

CHAPTER 4

*R*eid stood at the edge of the dock and stared at the lights flickering on the back of the sailboat. Little fish darted back and forth in the water. Darcie had taken him out on a catamaran once, and at first, he'd thought: *what on earth does this feisty little chick know about handling a vessel at sea.*

Boy, had she put him in his place.

While he was by no means an expert sailor—actually, he knew almost nothing—but because of the nature of his need for all things extreme, he'd been on the high seas a time or two.

However, spending a day with Darcie on the open water had opened his eyes, his mind, his soul, and his heart.

It took a fair amount of pizzazz to impress Reid,

and Darcie had done it in spades.

"Stalking me?" Her sweet voice rolled through his ears and slid down his throat, coating his stomach with the most decadent flavor. Who knew sound could be so tasty?

"Not you, the boat. I saw you get off here, and with the name and all, I assumed she was yours."

"That's a lot of dangerous surmising for a man who likes facts and nothing but the facts."

"I'm also a man who likes to live on the edge, so this is me being wild and out of control." He shrugged his shoulders and leaned against the post. The last time he'd seen her had been a random meeting in New Orleans that hadn't gone well at all.

At least, what he remembered of it. Honestly, it had been an encounter he'd prefer to forget.

She laughed. "I bought her a few months ago. When I'm not on a charter, I live on her."

"I was surprised to see you, and even more shocked you're running charters out of Seattle and not some exotic port. It's not like you to be in a mundane city such as this one."

"I wanted to be close to home for a bit." She waggled her index finger under his nose. "And don't you go knocking my hometown, or I'll start picking on your Southern drawl, Mr. Texas."

"You always loved when I got all cowboy on you

and did the two-step." He looped his fingers into his belt buckle and did a little kick with his feet.

She laughed, shaking her head.

He couldn't help but wonder if she was lying about wanting to be close to home, or if the family had put the pressure on. While she was tight with her siblings, she struggled with being overwhelmed by anyone encroaching on her space.

Something he could relate to.

When he'd last seen her, she'd been in New Orleans with her brother, visiting an old friend.

It looked more like a pity vacation, and she'd looked like shit.

Not that he'd looked any better. He had gone to Bourbon Street with one thing in mind: to get shit-faced every night and try to forget that Darcie ever existed. He'd thought he'd been hallucinating when she rounded the corner. He'd actually poked her in the center of the chest to see if she were real.

Jagar hadn't liked that.

Her friend, Asher, liked it even less.

Reid rubbed his jaw. "The last time I saw you, I said some things I shouldn't have."

"I'm surprised you even remember that day."

"A lot of it's still fuzzy, and that is both embarrassing and sucky as well as a bit of a saving grace at times." He let out a sarcastic chuckle. "But I owe you, your brother, and his friend a huge apology."

"Yeah. You do," she said. "And for more than just being a jerk in New Orleans. Your list of transgressions is long."

"I guess I walked into that one," he said, running a hand through his hair. "We both made mistakes in our relationship."

"Some of us made more than others."

"Wow. You're just not letting go of any of it, are you?" He tossed his hands to his sides, slapping his thighs.

"Sorry. You're the last person I expected to see. You kind of ruined my plans this week with this charter."

"What plans? Did you have a hot date? Are you seeing someone? In a long-term, committed relationship?"

"Wow. And what if I am?"

"Are you?" he asked.

"No. But I did have plans."

"Doing what, exactly? Because isn't being on charter what you live for?" He groaned. "Sorry. Old habits die hard."

"I guess they do," she said. "I'm taking the written portion of my captain's test next week. I wanted to use this time to study. You ruined that for me," she said.

"I'm shocked you haven't already taken it. You wanted to be a captain by now when we were together."

"Another thing you fucked up for me."

"How am I responsible for you not taking your test?"

"You're not." She huffed. "Other than it took me a little while to get my head on straight after we broke up."

"I can relate to that," he said. "I'm sure you'll ace it. You'll make a great captain." He desperately wanted to pull her into his arms, hold her close to his chest and kiss her sweet, tender lips. Letting her go had been the dumbest thing he'd ever done.

No. Telling her to leave her career had been.

"You didn't have that much faith in me when we were a couple." She wrapped one arm around her middle and brought her thumb to her mouth. She swayed back and forth.

That always drove him mad with desire. "Yes, I did."

"Really? Because near the end of our relationship, I seem to remember you telling me that my job was a waste of time and energy."

"I didn't mean it."

"Then you shouldn't have said it."

"I just didn't want you gone all the time. It's not easy to have a relationship with a woman whose job has her in exotic places with hot, sexy bodies surrounding her all the time. I'm generally not the type to get jealous, but you seemed more interested in your career than me, and it started to get to me."

"Now wait one second." She poked his biceps. "You told me you didn't think I was cut out to be a yachtie."

"No. I said you were in the business for the wrong reasons and that needed to stop. Said you needed to quit trying to prove you were good enough, and to either do it or get out." He held up his hand. This was not what he'd come here for, and he needed to go into tomorrow on basically the same page as Darcie. "I wanted to apologize, and I did. But I need to talk to you about something else. Can we go somewhere?"

"I don't know. I'm tired. I'm a little tipsy, as you can tell since I'm quick to temper. Can it wait until tomorrow?"

"No. It can't." He took her by the forearm and led her onto her boat. He'd spent the last few hours contemplating if he wanted to tell her anything. By doing so, he was really putting her in an awkward situation, and that was really fucking unfair—and an asshole move on his part. Apologizing to her didn't make up for it either. "I'm sorry, and you know I don't believe in this kind of crap, but maybe things do happen for a reason." He was all alone and had no one to turn to at this point. If he didn't shut Preston down, Reid ran the risk of losing it all. He didn't believe Preston was just going behind Reid's back with a new product.

No.

Reid couldn't help but wonder if Preston was making a run for the company. It shouldn't surpise Reid. Hell, it was something Reid had thought about doing to Preston a few years ago.

Only, Reid wouldn't be so underhanded about it.

The only question was how and when. And Reid needed a few days to figure out exactly what the fuck Preston was up to.

Darcie was an opportunity that had landed in his lap. No one could fault him for what he was about to do. Not in the long run.

"If you're going to say that you chartering the vessel I work on is a good thing, I'm going to absolutely disagree. You broke my heart. You called me a selfish bitch and humiliated me in front of the people I work with. And by the way,"—she leaned closer and poked his chest—"you should know that

Captain Jim is commanding the yacht. And up until about a month ago, I was sleeping with him."

"You and Jim? You've got to be fucking kidding me." He rubbed where her finger had bruised his body. She always found the most sensitive spots and then managed to get him with the sharpest side of her nail.

"I'm dead serious. But he's supposed to be getting engaged tonight to someone who used to be my friend." She patted Reid's arm. "I have shit taste in men who like to do horrible things to me."

"Come on, you should have known Jim would cheat. He's never been faithful to anyone, which is why I'm shocked he's getting married. Is she holding a gun to his head?"

"No. He really loves her," Darcie said, letting out a long breath. "Or so he says."

"I'm sorry about what Jim did. And I've said I'm sorry about what I did." He let out a puff of air. "I'm not helping my case here, but you broke my heart too. So, don't go playing innocent in our breakup. I'm taking a lot of the blame because I did put the final nail in our coffin. But you enjoyed tossing dirt on it."

"That was poetic," she mumbled. "I sure know how to pick the assholes."

"Hey, I never cheated on you," he said. "Got

anything to drink around this place?" He made himself comfortable on the aft deck, which was quite roomy. "This is what, a fifty-footer?"

"It is, and I'm really tired, Reid. If we keep going, it appears we've both had just enough to drink to piss each other off, so can we just call it a night?"

He rubbed his temples. She knew how to push all his buttons, the good ones and the bad ones, simultaneously.

"Reid. I accept your apology, and I make my own for tonight. My family was in rare form with the razzing, and my dad mentioned you, and he doesn't even know you're here. I'm just dealing with a lot."

"You read too much into what your parents say about your career. You always have."

"It gets hard when everyone around says the same thing."

"I'm going to run the risk of having you toss a shoe at me, but that's not true. The people in yachting that give you shit are either idiots who think they are motivating you, or are those afraid of you. Your folks just see the same thing I do."

"I'm not lost. I'm not running. I'm not hiding."

"Maybe not. However, you refuse to take a good look at what really makes you happy." He tilted his head and stared at the stars. There were so many things he wanted to say now that he had a clear head and a year to think about what was important. "I'm really sorry. The things I said that day in the Bahamas was totally uncalled for. I was hurt and angry. I was trying to do something nice for my girl-friend, and I felt completely unappreciated."

She turned, showing off her profile. Her pink tongue darted out of her mouth and stretched across her lips like a paintbrush leaving a glitter trail.

"When you were walking away with Preston, I kept hoping you'd turn around. But you didn't."

"We didn't speak to each other again until New Orleans," he said. "One beer. Let me talk to you for as long as it takes me to finish a single can." He tilted his head. "Please?"

"Fine. But when it's gone, you're gone." She disappeared into the galley.

He peeked inside the cabin. The fine teak wood was accented with a dark brown, high-end vinyl upholstery. She certainly had good taste, that was for damn sure. He could only imagine what this thing cost her, and it was probably killing her financially to maintain it between the marina fees and whatever else went into living on a boat. "Do you really like being here? Isn't it kind of small? Or creepy late at night."

"It's never creepy on the water. And small? No. Not when it's just me. And I love to go out and sail.

I've gone all the way up to Alaska, down to Mexico, and I wouldn't mind taking some other trips." She handed him a beer while she nursed a bottle of water. She sat next to him, tucking her feet up under her cute little ass. Her hair caught in the gentle breeze, blowing it over her shoulders. The moonlight threaded through the natural blond highlights, making her hair glow.

The massive wheel stood proudly in the center of the back deck. He could envision her standing behind it with one hand covering her eyes as the sails grew tight with the wind, and the boat hugged the water.

When they first met, her age had bothered him. She'd been so young and had yet to experience even half of what life had to offer. Only he'd been wrong about what she understood about life. And what the hell was in a number anyway? Twelve years wasn't that big of a deal at this point in their lives.

"This sailboat fits you," he said.

"Thanks." She held his gaze for a long moment. She could still take his breath away with her powder blue eyes. She had thick, long lashes, and when she blinked, he bit down on his lower lip in anticipation of when they'd flutter open again, showing off those intoxicating orbs. "What have you been up to for the last year?"

"Work, mostly." He could have been honest and told her that he'd spent the first six months of it drunk and unaware of anything. That he'd become a useless human being because he'd let her walk out of his life.

And she didn't come back and fight for him.

After that, as his brain slowly came out of its fog, he'd found out that his friend and business partner had been doing his best to make sure Reid would get nothing of their company. In reality, Reid had only put it all together in the last few weeks, and Reid wasn't even sure he'd uncovered half of it.

Which terrified him.

He knew Preston could be ruthless. They always joked that they were the perfect team because Reid always knew when to pull back and keep Preston from becoming his own worst enemy.

Reid, though a sports extremist, didn't take certain types of risks, and that's where Preston came in. He was willing to go into the shark-infested deep end with both feet and his eyes closed while doused in blood.

But somewhere along the way, Preston had gone all lone wolf.

"I heard you were on that television show where inventors go and ask rich people for money. Kind of funny when you're independently wealthy."

"Not rich enough to do everything I want." Reid laughed. "I didn't go on the show because I wanted to. It was all part of the movie contract, which is all Preston's baby. I would have rather said no. I'm still bitter about it. And I'm not supposed to say anything, but they turned us down."

"Is that good or bad?"

"It doesn't really matter. Preston got his deal with the production company. He gets to move forward with my product and design when I'm not even sure it's ready."

"So, Preston still manages to manipulate you to get his way, I see."

"It's a balancing act. You know that. I toss him a bone, and I get what really matters."

"Right. You're a crusader trying to make sure people don't get hurt while using faulty equipment in search of some ridiculous thrill, all in the name of a dead woman."

"I was a safety nut before Erin died. You know that." Reid had never really pushed back too hard when Erin came up in conversations. He let Darcie think he used her death to protect his heart. It wasn't entirely a lie. "Her death just pushed me into taking our idea that was only in the beginning stages in a whole new direction."

"One that Preston didn't like."

"He liked it and still does, he just doesn't want it to be the focal point because it doesn't bring in the highest revenue."

"I don't think you came here to talk to me about this shit."

"Nope." Reid took a sip, swirling the bubbles of the beer around in his mouth. He couldn't tell her everything or even half of what he suspected. But he needed to get into some files without Preston knowing, and that required some help. "I need a huge favor." Reid hadn't given this a ton of thought, and he wasn't sure it would work at all, but it was his best bet, given the time constraints and the fact that Preston might be three sheets to the wind for the next three days.

"I told you, my brother—"

He shook his head and held up his hand. "I don't give a fuck about that bungee jump. I'm really not into that shit anymore." He chuckled. "Well, I am, but not like I used to be. However, I'm really not concerned with whether or not we get to do that night free fall."

"Then what do you need my help with?" The wind kicked up and took a stray strand of hair, flicking it across her face.

He reached out and tucked it behind an ear. "I

need the internet to go down on the boat, but not really."

"Excuse me?"

"I need Preston and the rest of the team blocked from using the WiFi for at least one day. Or I need a secondary WiFi set up where I'm the only one who has access to it. I can help you set it up."

"Why?"

"I need to cut off communication between Preston and the company."

"He will still have cell reception."

"That's not going to matter for what I need to do," Reid said. "We'll do it during the kayak trip to the rapids. I'll pretend to be so drunk that I can't go. We both know I can get so shitfaced I'm utterly useless."

"I won't argue that point."

"Can you help me with this?" Another swig. He closed one eye, peering into the can. About half full.

That sucked. Not only did he enjoy Darcie's company, but the idea of going back to his hotel room made him want to vomit. When he'd been with Darcie, some of their best nights had been spent sleeping under the stars on a boat somewhere in the middle of a body of water.

Any body of water would do where she was concerned.

"Which would you prefer? No WiFi for your buddies? Or your own login? Either way, I'm going to need some help on the boat to make that happen," she said, twirling her hair between her fingers—something she did when she was relaxed.

Much better than making her nervous.

"I mean just unplugging the router and taking the cord won't work because they will have more. It's all on our checklist."

"That will also cut me off from the WiFi," he said rubbing his temple with his free hand. "All you need to do is show me were the routers are, and I'll take care of it." He could handle hacking into the boat's system. What he couldn't handle was accessing the secondary server without Preston finding out—or so he thought. But he'd continue wracking his brain until he figured it out.

"I'm confused on what you want me to do," she said, tilting her head. "What are you trying to accomplish?"

"I need Preston and my team off the internet while I do some research."

"About what?"

"I can't give you all the details."

"You want me to help you, but you're going to keep me in the dark? It doesn't work that way."

"It's for your own protection," he said.

"What can you tell me?" she asked, bringing her water bottle to her plump, pink, kissable lips. "I can't just do you a solid without having some intel."

"I think one of the men on my team is stealing from the company. And before I bring it to Preston, I want to make sure I have all the facts."

"You expect me to believe that?" She leaned forward, putting both elbows on her knees. "And I still don't understand the internet thing."

"I need you to trust me. If I go digging into certain things, Preston will get an email and a text that I'm poking around in employee files, and he'll wonder why. And I don't have a very good poker face when it comes to this shit. I don't want the vibe on the boat to be anything but the team getting drunk and having a good time, outside of the work that Preston and I will make them do. Because you know, we don't ever stop." Fuck. He hated lying to Darcie. Not just because she despised dishonest people but also because he loathed doing the one thing she'd begged him never to do. Ever, no matter what.

Not that she'd ever forgive him for being the biggest dickhead on the planet. Darcie was a reasonable woman, but she didn't tolerate old-fashioned misogynistic bullshit like her boyfriend telling her that being a yacht captain was a man's career. To this day, he cringed every time he thought about the words he'd used when he tried to beg her to reconsider her choices so they could be together.

Of course, looking back, he realized that he hadn't done much in the way of offering to change his lifestyle for her, something he should have put some thought into.

But what was done was done. And right now, he needed to focus on his company.

When that was done, he could work on getting Darcie back in his life. Because he was still head over heels in love with her.

There was no doubt about that. She still tickled his fancy, pushed all the right buttons, and if there were ever the perfect adrenaline rush, it would be called *The Darcie*.

"I just need access to your router. That's all."

"It's not going to be easy because the router is housed in the cockpit, and Captain Jim doesn't like guests up there unless he's there to supervise."

"Please tell me you were kidding when you said you fucked around with Captain Jim."

"I could tell you that but it would be a lie."

Cold goosebumps dotted his skin. "Jesus. Seriously? You and Jim? I'm just not picturing it. You used to warn the female deckhands and all the stews to stay away from all-hands Captain Jim. I mean, he's not a horrible human being, but as a man, he kind of falls short."

"Well, it doesn't matter. I wasn't joking when I said he's in love with someone else and is getting engaged tonight."

"Ouch."

"Not really," she said. "I didn't love him. I'm just mad that, once again, I'm the last to know that my boyfriend just isn't that into me."

Reid narrowed his eyes. "Was that a jab at me? Because I'll have you know, I was all sorts of into you when we were together. The only reason we broke up was because I wanted a girlfriend who wasn't gone more than two hundred days out of the year."

"That's not exactly how you put it."

"If I had used those words, would we still be together?"

She shook her head. "The moment you asked me to choose between you and my dreams and everything that I'd been working toward, that was the moment you lost me."

"If it makes you feel any better, I know I was wrong."

"It doesn't," she said. "But that's all in the past. We've both moved forward."

Maybe she had, but he was still stuck in a land of

fantasy where she would forgive him and welcome him back with open arms.

And he'd focus on that. Just as soon as he got rid of fucking Preston, something he should have done years ago.

Reid swallowed his heartburn. His life hadn't turned out quite as he'd planned. "I'm sorry I hurt you. I really am."

"Apology accepted."

He polished off the last of his beer. "I guess I better be going." He stood, placing the empty can in the recycling bin. "Thanks for the time and for your help. I owe you."

"I'm sure someday I'll think of a way you can repay me." She closed the gap between them and rested her hands on his shoulders. "Good night, Reid."

"Good night, Darcie," he said, pressing his lips to her cheek. He let them linger on her hot skin longer than appropriate, and she didn't stop him from taking her into his arms and heaving her body to his chest. "I don't want to leave."

"Then don't."

* * *

HOLY. Fucking. Shit.

Darcie shoved her tongue deep into Reid's mouth, touching every crevice. She found every spicy hot spot, making him moan as he grabbed her ass, squeezing tightly, leaving deep impressions.

Gripping his shoulders, she meant to push him away, only a major dose of insanity took over her brain and she tugged him into the galley.

She'd lost her fucking mind, but she didn't fucking care.

The boat swayed gently as the water lapped against the fiberglass. The lines rattled the mast, and somewhere in the distance, a woman laughed, and music hummed.

The inside of her boat consisted of a tiny kitchen that encroached into her living room, and a small bedroom with a surprisingly comfortable queen-size bed. She'd broken the bank with this purchase, but it had been her dream for so long. Sailing had always been a passion. The sea was in her blood. It calmed her and gave her a sense of freedom.

The water gave her courage and strength.

She was at her happiest when the ocean tickled at least one of her senses. The only other time in her life that she'd had that kind of security was when Reid had been in her bed.

She jerked her head back.

He blinked. His thick tongue darted out of his

mouth, making a broad stroke across his tantalizing lips.

She heaved in a deep breath. Her lungs burned as she tried to form words. "What are we doing?"

"Probably making a big mistake." He fiddled with a strand of her hair. "But you know me. I don't like to leave things unfinished once I start them."

"I've had a little too much to drink."

"Do I need to be worried that I could be taking advantage of you?"

She smiled. "No. I'm definitely in control of all my faculties, and I'm definitely going to regret this in the morning." She took a step back, her butt hitting the small table. She fiddled with the buttons on her blouse, unhooking the top two.

He pressed his hands against the counter at her hips, easing himself between her legs. "As much as I want you right now,"—he gripped her wrist—"I'm not going to stay."

She groaned, dropping her head to his shoulder. "I lied. I'm regretting throwing myself at you now. No need to wait till morning."

"It would have been worse if one of us didn't come to our senses." He continued running his tender, loving hands up and down her back.

She sighed.

"Are you okay?"

"In one night, I get rejected by one ex and find out another is going to propose to a woman who I was planning to teach how to sail when this charter season was over. I actually made a female friend in yachting, only to find her on top of Jim's dick."

"Figuratively, right?"

"No. I literally walked in on them. It was ugly. I made a scene."

"Wait. Don't tell me this was during a charter?" He kissed the center of her chest before buttoning her shirt. Resting his hands on her hips, he rubbed gently. He could be really sweet in the oddest moments.

But when she'd needed his support the most, he'd acted like a spoiled, selfish child.

"We had a couple of days off. She'd left the bar early, saying she didn't feel well. I was worried, so I went back to the boat to check on her and see Jim. I never thought they were fucking. She was actually the only one who knew about me and Jim. I felt like a total idiot, and I was also a little drunk and lost my shit. I'm lucky I didn't get fired."

"Jim's lucky he's still a captain."

"It was a hot mess. And truth be told, we all could have been told to take a hike. But Kim quit that morning, and whatever she said to the powers that be saved all our asses. Though there are times I wish I had tossed them under the bus."

Reid shook his head and pursed his lips. It was the same look he'd given her when she did something he disapproved of, and it made her want to smack the back side of his head.

"What?" she asked.

"Did you threaten to have her fired?"

"No. Just him. And trust me, I've contemplated doing it, but I'd end up losing my rank as boson, so it's just not worth it." She fingered the hair hugging the back of Reid's neck. It should feel weird to be so comfortable in his arms. It was like that perfect wetsuit that molded to your body and no one else's.

She waffled on the verge of a raging river filled with an angry current, wanting to continue lashing out at him so he knew just how much he'd hurt her...and a flowery meadow with a slight breeze, bringing the scents of summer to her nose.

There certainly was a fine line between love and hate.

"I'm sorry he cheated on you. That sucks, and you deserve better."

"I do." She wiped away some of her lip gloss that had managed to make its way to his cheek. "Do you have a girlfriend? Is that why you're refusing me?"

The one thing Reid could always be called was honorable. He'd never cheat. Not in a million years.

"No girlfriend. And trust me, I'm not rejecting you." He cupped her face. "Maybe when the charter's over, we can go get a bite to eat? Talk? See where we are?"

"Are you still living in Houston?"

He chuckled. "Actually, this city cowboy moved out to Galveston Island. And get this. I live on the water."

"I'm shocked. Do you take the time to sit still and enjoy it?"

He kissed her nose. "I've even read a book." He took a step back and stuffed his hands into his pockets. "I better leave before I get into my *fuck it and go for it* attitude, which I told myself I wouldn't toss to the wind until I was forty. And I haven't hit that mark yet."

"You're not that far off, old man."

"Thanks for the reminder." He winked. "I really appreciate your help, and please don't say anything to Preston. You know how he gets."

"Don't worry. I've got your back…" The last word hung in the air. A thick lump grew in her throat. There was a time when the only person who really understood her, the one that would be there for her at the snap of a finger, had been Reid.

He used to tell her all the time that no matter where in the world she traveled, he'd always have her back.

"I'm glad we had this time to chat," he said. "I'll see myself out."

"Good night, Reid." She watched as he made his way onto the dock and strolled down toward the marina.

He glanced over his shoulder five times.

She knew that for a fact because she counted.

The sex had always been good. Great. The best she'd ever had. And he'd told her that making love to her had been the ultimate extreme experience for him. It had been the most hysterical and yet most romantic moment of her life.

She closed the door, locked it, and ditched her clothes for a pair of boxers and a tank top. When it came to the WiFi situation, she had two choices. Either ask Jim to help her, or Kirk or Craig.

It had to be Jim. He wouldn't like it, because he didn't like Reid much, but Jim owed her. And based on Reid's plea for help, it was the least she could do for an old friend.

She pulled up Asher's contact information.

Darcie: If you're up, give me a call. If not, call me first thing. Thanks.

A second later, her phone vibrated. She snagged

her water bottle and flopped onto her bed as she answered the call. "That was quick."

"Anything for my favorite fill-in babysitter. How goes the yachtie life?"

"It's going," she said. "How's Casey?"

"She's doing great, and so is Lilia. Now, what's wrong, kiddo? Because you don't go texting me late in the evening for no reason."

"I can't check in with an old friend?"

"No. You can't. And before I forget, I'm actually in Seattle."

"What? When did you get here?" She rolled to her side and fiddled with her penguin pillow.

The one Reid had won for her at a stupid carnival on their very first official date.

"I just got off a plane two hours ago. And before you ask, I flew solo. I'm here for a cop thing."

"I just saw my brother. He didn't tell me you were coming."

"I was sent to the conference last-minute. The person who was supposed to go got sick, and I offered. Casey and Lilia will come for the weekend."

"Sweet. I have Sunday off. I'll take you all out on my sailboat," Darcie said.

"It's a date. Now, what's got your panties in a wad?"

"If someone wanted to bungee jump off a bridge, what would they have to do?"

"Just do it before anyone finds out and hope to God no one gets hurt. But that would be a moronic thing to do."

"I'm talking about a professional stunt person or a sports extremist. Whose palm would they have to grease in this city to make that happen off a bridge or tower where a recreational thrill company isn't offering jumps to regular people?"

"They need something similar to a special use or a production permit that filming companies apply for. Those are given out by the town and county, depending on the details. It usually takes a while to get one. Why are you asking? And please don't tell me it has anything to do with the asshole I smacked in the chin."

"You shouldn't have hit him. He was drunk. And you, Jagar, and Matt were all being assholes."

"So was your ex-boyfriend. And for the record, he started it."

"No. Jagar started it when he got in Reid's face and called him a douchebag for breaking up with me. And Reid felt the need to tell Jagar why it was a mutual breakup."

"It went a little deeper and harsher than that, and you know it."

Darcie snuggled up to the porthole and watched the waterline gently bobble against the glass. The sounds of the lines rattling against the mast and the seagulls crying above gave her peace of mind.

But she still had a restless soul.

Both her older brothers could be overwhelmingly protective at times. As a little girl, she couldn't wait for Jagar to get the hell out of the house. He was the worst, always checking out her boyfriends and doing background checks on the people she hung out with.

He was worse than her parents most of the time.

"Why do you want to help Reid out with this, and why is he in Seattle?"

"I just found out he's my charter tomorrow. He had no idea. It's a celebration with his business partner. So, it's my job to help make this happen if I can."

"Well, if he's going for Deception Pass, it won't happen. Sorry, kiddo. I can make a call if you want me to, but the chances are slim to none."

"Thanks. I appreciate it."

"No problem," Asher said. "I want you to know I wasn't proud of myself the day I clocked Reid. But you're family, and I won't tolerate anyone hurting those I care about."

"You're simply the best." She pulled the sheets over her body and settled in, holding onto the pillow. It would be weird being around Reid for three days and two nights.

But it might be good, too.

The second she closed her eyes, an image of Reid in a pair of shorts, flip-flops, and no shirt appeared in her mind. Even though they'd never be a couple again, she could let go of the anger she'd burned into her heart. She had to make this a turning point in her life.

CHAPTER 5

*R*eid stared at the screen and blinked. His fingers trembled. He glanced around the hotel room until his gaze fixed on the window. The first curve of the yellow sun kissed the light blue sky. A fifty-million-dollar business with one hundred direct employees, and he couldn't trust a fucking single one.

Why?

Because he'd had a stupid breakdown over Darcie.

He slammed his fist on the sofa and jumped to his feet. Pacing at the edge of the bed and planting his hands on his hips, he let out a long breath. He had no right to be mad at her for his inability to get over her. That wasn't her fault. He should have fought for her. He should have told her that he would have followed her to the ends of the Earth.

Instead, he'd ruined his life.

"Fuck," he muttered. He had to get into the backup server without Preston being notified, and he wasn't sure how he could do that since he no longer knew the external password. The only way for him to get into the system was to do it from inside.

But that would alert Preston.

Reid was fucked.

And once Preston got wind that Reid was poking around... God only knew what his partner might do or how he would respond.

The worst part was that Reid was pretty fucking sure that Preston was up to more than sliding the fire-retardant material into manufacturing early. Reid just didn't know *what,* and he wasn't sure how to find the answers. What he did know was that he hated putting Darcie right smack dab in the middle of it all.

His cell phone buzzed.

A text from Preston indicating a change in plans and that there would be no jump off Deception Pass.

Thank God.

That was the last thing Reid wanted to do, only he didn't like the replacement excursion very much either. He'd rather double down on the kayaking through the rapids.

His chosen ring tone chimed. He jumped.

A local number that he didn't recognize appeared on the screen. He declined the call and tossed his phone onto the bed. He had to figure out how to get into the system without Preston being notified. It shouldn't be this hard. It was like an alarm, so maybe he could intercept the texts somehow.

No. That wouldn't work because he had no clue how to do that. He considered himself well-versed in technology and knew a thing or two more than most, but he wasn't that good.

His phone rang out again.

Same local number.

He figured he better answer it this time.

"Hello?"

"Hi, Reid. It's Jagar Bowie."

Of all the people in Seattle, Jagar was not someone Reid expected to hear from. "Hey, Jagar. What can I do for you?"

"I was hoping to meet you for a cup of coffee this morning."

"I'm going to be getting on a boat shortly."

"I know. My sister's vessel," Jagar said with quite the stern, deep voice. "But that's not till noon, and the marina is across the street. I'm in the lobby. If I don't see you in five, I'll be up banging on your door."

"Isn't this something like police harassment?" Reid said sarcastically under his breath.

"If I didn't sort of like you, I'd take offense."

"I'll be down in a few." Reid stuffed his phone into his pocket along with the plastic key. He slipped his feet into his cowboy boots and meandered out the door. If he had a little sister, he'd be doing the same thing. He couldn't blame Jagar for being concerned.

When they first met, Jagar had really disliked Reid, in part because of Reid's age. He wondered what a man a little older than him would see in his kid sister. But after spending some time together, Jagar and Reid had become good friends.

Until the breakup.

Reid stepped from the elevator and found Jagar sitting at one of the tables in the breakfast area with two tall mugs of coffee. He didn't wear a cop uniform, but he had a badge hanging on his navy-blue shirt and gun on his hip.

"I really didn't think I'd see you this trip." Reid held out his arm.

Jagar shook his hand good and hard. "You're looking much better than the last time our paths crossed."

"Yeah, that's a night I wish never happened." Reid took a seat and shifted. "The things I do remember were pretty rotten, and what I don't remember I wish people would stop filling me in on." He glanced inside the mug and smiled. "You remembered."

"For a Southern man who claims to be a fucking cowboy, you drink coffee like a goddamned girl with all that fancy-schmancy stuff. And I'm not sure I got it right. The girl at the coffee shop didn't understand one of the things I said, so she did the best on what she thought I meant."

"It smells like it's got all my requirements." He brought the paper mug to his lips and closed his eyes. "Oh. That's good fucking coffee. Darcie won't have that on her yacht. I'll have to suffer for a few days."

"How did that happen, by the way?"

"What? Me ending up on your sister's boat?" Reid shrugged. "Pure luck. Never in a million years would I have believed Darcie would wind up back here of all places. She swore to me she'd never live in Seattle. Ever. Not even to have a slip for a boat."

"Don't take this the wrong way, but after the two of you broke up, she went a little crazy. Coming home was the first sane thing she did, though we all thought it weird and very unlike her. She tends to run away when things get tough, not come crawling home."

"I agree, which is why I was shocked. Do you know what she has planned after this summer season?"

"She's taking her captain's test. But after that, she doesn't have anything lined up. Another scary thing for the family."

"She's gone weeks, even a month between gigs before."

"But she's always had them ready and waiting. We know she wants to captain, but she's not even looking." Jagar leaned back, resting his hand on the butt of his weapon.

Reid pinched the bridge of his nose. "Why am I here?" This was not the type of conversation he'd envisioned when he walked into this lobby.

"Two reasons. First, I'm asking you to stay away from Deception Pass. Don't make me arrest you."

"I've always enjoyed handcuffs."

Jagar rolled his eyes.

"Don't worry. We have called off those plans." Reid held up his hands. "Swear to God. We're going looking for sharks instead, or at least that's what Preston says we're doing."

"Are you being strainght with me?"

"I'm telling you what *I'm* being told. But either way, I'm not participating. I've got bigger fish to fry."

"At least I won't have to pull your body from the water," Jagar said. "The second reason I'm here is my sister. I know there are two sides to every breakup, and seeing you in New Orleans, I can tell Darcie did a number on you. And I'm not sold that either of you are over the other." Jagar held up his hand, waving his wedding ring. "My wife and I had a horrible breakup after I told her that I put the wrong person behind bars, and a killer struck again, murdering my wife's sister. So, I know a little about heartache and patching that sucker back up."

Reid knew all this, and he sure as shit didn't want to sit here and listen to it again when he needed to figure out how to save his company and get Preston the fuck out of his life. However, he couldn't be rude to Jagar. It wouldn't be right.

"I shouldn't be the one telling you this, but Darcie spent the first part of this year working every exotic boat she could get on. She even took a job as a stew again."

"Oh, good grief, she did not." Reid struggled to see Darcie working on the interior of a yacht. Besides it being stereotypical, something Darcie couldn't stand, it was not the kind of work she was good at.

"It was as if she was trying to work you out of her system. And then Captain Jim hired her as boson on a yacht. Next thing we knew, she and Slimy Jim were an item."

"I take it you don't like Captain Jim," Reid said with his hand over his mouth, trying to contain his amusement.

"He cheated on my sister."

"Yes. I know that," Reid said, clearing his throat.

Jagar lowered his gaze. "How?"

"Darcie told me last night."

"She said she ran into you for like ten minutes. I'm surprised she told you about Jim at all." Jagar squeezed his paper mug and tossed it into the garbage.

"I was still at the docks when she got back from your parents' house."

"Really. And what happened?"

"Nothing," Reid said. "She and I just needed to clear the air. I wanted to apologize. That's it."

Jagar stood and adjusted his pants, looping his fingers into his weapons belt. "Do you still love my sister?"

"Interesting question when you're standing in cop mode, presenting your gun as if I'm being inter-rogated." In order to level the playing field, Reid hopped to his feet.

"It's just a simple question."

"That has a complicated answer. And a man who's had his heart crushed by the woman he loves more than life itself should understand that."

"I guess I have my answer." Jagar smiled. "The one thing my family, especially my father, doesn't understand about Darcie is that she's not running or chasing anything. While they are all trying to figure out what it is she wants. Or why she wants it. And suffocating her while doing it. She's living the dream, only no one who matters to her ever gave her permission to enjoy it."

Reid opened his mouth. Nothing but a gasp came out. He closed it and tried again. "That was profound and kind of beautifully said."

"I'm married to a writer, who has me read and write with her these days. I find myself saying weird shit all the time. But even I didn't get it until my father said something last night about Darcie, and it hit me that we're all asking her to conform to what *we* think, and no one is listening to what *she* thinks. She always used to say being the baby sucked because everyone knew things before she did. She hated it when any of us said something like *'you just wait until you're my age.'*"

"Try being twelve years older and her boyfriend and say something like that." Reid palmed his coffee mug. "She's always felt like she had to fight to be seen, heard, and respected in anything she's ever done."

A young couple, who were barely awake, and their two toddlers, who were bright-eyed and bushy-tailed, entered the breakfast area. The young mother mumbled something about birth control and caffeine, while the father waggled a finger, and the kids and pretended to scold them.

When he was Darcie's age, or even Jagar's age, Reid didn't think he wanted a wife, let alone kids. He didn't want to settle down. He liked jet-setting from one whirlwind adventure to the next.

And then he went and fell in love with Erin. She was a bright soul with dark demons. However, she made him want to be a better version of himself, and if she could have gotten a handle on her emotional and mental issues, well, he really didn't know. Because she wasn't here anymore.

But Darcie was flesh and blood, and she'd turned his world upside down and shook him to the core. He went from wanting to be thrown from a rocket as a human bullet to sitting on a front porch with a puppy, a newspaper, and maybe, just maybe, a little boy or girl playing in the front yard. And then she'd walked out of his life, and she'd taken the image with her.

"I know. As her big brother, it pains me to see her struggle like that and not be able to dropkick her so she gets that she's her own worst enemy."

"Sometimes, we have to figure that one out for ourselves." Reid scratched the back of his head. He'd stood in the way of himself for years after Erin died. He couldn't open himself up because he always worried that once he peeled back a layer, he'd find the ugly demons.

But everyone had a past.

Baggage.

He'd learned when he fell in love with Darcie that he hadn't been afraid of losing someone again, but rather of not being able to save them. Because no matter what he did, he knew he never would have been able to fix Erin.

She knew it too, and in the end, she did what she believed—no, what she *knew*—would end the suffering for everyone.

Darcie had been right, and in the beginning of their relationship, he used Erin's death as a shield. And that had been a shitty thing to do. By the time he figured it out and tried to turn things around, it was too late. Darcie already had one foot out the door.

"What's on your mind?" Jagar asked.

"Just work stuff. I really shouldn't be taking a

three-day cruise. But my partner is still more like a twenty-year-old surfer dude than a grown-ass man."

"I've heard Preston is a piece of work." Jagar glanced over his shoulder as the two toddlers knocked over a thing of milk. He covered his mouth. "I'm going to suck at being a father because I won't be able to keep a straight face when my kid does stuff like that."

"I'm sure you'll be a great one. Thanks for stopping by. It was really good to see you."

"You too, man." Jagar slapped Reid on the shoulder. "Tell my sister you still love her and then listen to what she has to say. That's all she wants. To be heard."

"Yes, oh wise man."

"And don't ever say that again." Jagar waved his hand over his head. "Have a fun trip. We'll see you for dinner at my place when you get back."

"I don't think so," Reid responded.

"You're going to sweep my sister off her feet." The doors closed behind Jagar.

"I'm probably going to get myself thrown off the ship by my own business partner, but that will be about the only excitement," he mumbled as he headed to the elevators and poked at the button.

It was going to be a long couple of days.

CHAPTER 6

*D*arcie sipped her coffee in the crew mess while Milia, the chief stew, and her second, Anastasia, finished putting away the provisions. Chef Haley prepared trays of appetizers for when the guests arrived. The hour before a charter was always the most stressful for the interior crew, but the deck staff wouldn't get too busy until the vessel pulled away.

Reid as a guest on her yacht. That was a surreal concept. He'd come to visit her many times while she worked a charter season in the two years they'd dated. Depending on the captain of the vessel, they either had to get a hotel room, or they could stay in the guest cabins on the yacht.

She found it ironic that it was Jim who always said no to Reid staying on the vessel.

"I heard you know these boys pretty well," Milia said with a bright smile.

Darcie had to have known that everyone on the boat would find out that she and Reid used to have a thing. The question was what they knew, and how fast the insanity spread. "What were you told and by whom?" She took the preference sheets of all the guests and scanned them. They had already gone over them with the captain, and Haley had a good handle on what Reid, Preston, and the rest of the team wanted in the food department. Preston could be a douchebag when it came to food. He constantly complained, and nothing was ever good enough, not even when he cooked it himself.

But what disturbed her was the missing bungee jump off Deception Pass on the activities list. In its place, they had them leaving the yacht at twenty-two hundred hours and going scuba diving. Why did they need to leave with someone else?

Because they decided to leave her and Jim out of the equation?

However, that really didn't exonerate them, or the boat owners from liability if something happened.

Her brother was going to have her head if she didn't tell him, but she wouldn't lose her job over that one.

"Don't get mad," Milia said, "but Kim told me this morning that Jim said you used to date the primary's business partner."

Darcie inhaled sharply, checking her temper. She wasn't really angry with Milia or Kim. Not really. Not anymore. Hell, she couldn't even stay pissed at Jim. The only person she was angry with was herself, and it was high time she stopped kicking herself over her bad choices and started learning from them and moving forward.

"That would be a true statement."

"I heard it was for like two years," Milia said.

"I thought Kim and Jim were getting engaged last night? Didn't they have better things to do than gossip about me?" She flicked her wrist, tossing out the last couple of swigs of her coffee in the sink. So much for turning over a new leaf and checking her sarcasm at the door.

"We're all just curious what the feel of the boat is going to be for the next three days." Haley, the chef, had always been the quietest person on the vessel. She didn't say much of anything, but when she did open her mouth, she was usually the voice of reason. "We've been walking on eggshells ever since Kim left, and to be frank, we're all kind of tired of it."

"No offense to anyone, but you should have all come at me with that upfront, instead of tiptoeing around the subject. Because it just makes me defensive and pissed off." She adjusted her ponytail. "Things could get awkward. And because of my history with both primaries, I could end up losing my cool if they get in my face."

Just as she said that, two of her deckhands came waltzing into the galley.

"Is someone giving you shit?" Kirk asked. "Because if they are, I'll kick their ass."

"Me, too." Bradley snagged a mug and made himself some coffee. "But what are we talking about?"

"Your boson's love life." Anastasia picked at a head of lettuce. She always liked helping in the kitchen, and she was a pretty good cook, often making the crew meals when Haley had a big dinner for the guests to deal with. But she could be a bit of a shit-stirrer, enjoying the conflict as long as she wasn't part of it. "And the fact that one of our guests is *the ex.*"

"Shit," Kirk mumbled. "The guy you were dating when we first worked together in Greece? The one you'd broken up with by the time we met again in Florida?"

"That's the one," she said. "His business partner, Preston, can be a bit of a dick, and he'll constantly try to get a rise out of me."

"Hey, sounds like he'll get along with the rest of us," Bradley said.

"You're going to hate Preston." Darcie shook her head. "He's a pretentious trust fund kid who doesn't understand the word *no*."

"And you dated his business partner?" Haley stopped chopping mushrooms and stared at Darcie.

Everyone had discontinued their activities and glared at her with their jaws dropped as if they were driving by a horrible accident and couldn't look away.

"You don't tolerate people like that," Bradley said, breaking the silence. "The way you pick on some of the guests after they leave is priceless. How could you date someone with stupid money?"

"Reid isn't like Preston, other than being an adrenaline junkie. They have very different personalities. Where the tension is going to be is between me and Preston more than me and Reid. Maybe. Probably."

"Toss Jim into the mix, and we've got ourselves some rough waters ahead," Kirk said.

"Hey, did anyone notice all the luggage he brought back on the vessel?" Bradley asked.

"I did." Kirk snapped open a soda. "I saw that he did that a couple of charters ago, too. But when I went looking for the bags, they were nowhere to be found."

"You actually go looking for his luggage," Darcie said. "That's weird."

"I only went looking because he brought all these extra things aboard the charter Kim ended up leaving. But when I went to get her bags, his were nowhere to be found. Later, I saw him leaving the vessel with them," Bradley said.

"Come to think of it, he brought on extra bags that disappeared on our first charter," Kirk said.

"Really fucking weird, if you ask me," Bradley said.

"Jim does have an obsession for clothes, and he always overpacks." Something that Darcie enjoyed poking fun at whenever she got the chance.

"All crew. All crew. Captain Jim here. I see our guests walking the gangway. Let's get this party started."

"You heard the man." Darcie smoothed down the front of her dark slacks. One thing she hated about this job was the constant changing of clothes. Right after they greeted the guests, she and the deck crew would change into their sun shirts and shorts and prepare the vessel to leave port, where they'd spend a couple of hours cruising up the coast until they found their anchor spot. And then they could break out the toys and let the drunken bad behavior begin.

She stood next to Captain Jim with her hands clasped behind her back.

"Are you ready for this?" Jim asked.

"Don't worry. Reid and I will be fine," she whispered.

"I'm more worried about you and Preston." Jim stretched out his arm. "Reid. It's good to see you again. And you as well, Preston. We look forward to making this short vacation special for you boys."

Preston cocked his head and arched his brow. "Make sure we have lots of tequila and food and we'll be good."

"Hey. How are you holding up?" Reid whispered as he kissed her cheek.

"Just ducky. How are you?"

"I'm peachier today."

She laughed.

"Jim's being awfully nice to me."

"He wants a big fat tip," she whispered, patting Reid's shoulder, trying to move him along.

Talk about fucking games. Jim had some really choice words for Reid the last time they'd seen each other. Of course, Darcie was acting like a fool and screaming at Reid because Reid had called her a selfish bitch who didn't have a clue about real love or life for that matter.

Darcie had learned one very valuable lesson since that day.

She had anger management issues, and finding Jim with her bunkmate made her understand that she really hadn't done anything to figure out how to deal with those kinds of emotions.

Well, she would start doing something about them today.

Besides, she didn't love Jim. Never had. She was better off without him.

Reid was an entirely different story.

One she'd have to come to terms with because even if they went to dinner when this charter was over and there was more than sex between them, she lived on a boat docked in Seattle, and he lived on an island off the coast of Texas.

It was a doomed relationship.

So why the fuck was she thinking about him in terms of getting back together?

The final guest came through the receiving line. Quickly, she gathered up all the luggage and had her crew change into their other uniform. Since they were nearing the end of this charter season, they had leaving the port down and left the dock without incident.

She meandered up to the bow of the vessel and inhaled the fresh salty sea air. She loved the first few minutes at sea. It was as if she were returning home from a long day at work.

Reid and the rest of the guests were lounging on the back patio being served drinks and appetizers and flirting with the interior crew.

That fine fucking line that made this job so much harder because everything was based on service and tip. At least she didn't have to worry about her flirty ways this trip.

Her crew was either resting or finishing a few other things on their day-one charter checklist.

The sound of bare feet scuffing across fiberglass caught her attention. She glanced over her shoulder. "Hey, Kirk."

"It amazes me that more guests don't find their way up here. It has to be the best place to hang out when we're cruising. Or even when we're anchored if you just want some peace and quiet."

"It's not necessarily an easy walk, especially when we're moving. And once you're here, there's nothing to do. The guests would rather be near the hot tub and the bar. Besides, it's our little paradise."

"It sure is." Kirk took a swig of water. "What are your plans when this season is over?"

"I don't know yet. It depends on my captain's test and a few other things."

"You just have the written portion left, correct?"

She nodded.

"Have you applied? Because I know a few owners looking for good captains."

"Thanks. I'll keep that in mind," she said.

"That brings me to why I flagged you down. Would it be okay if I put you down as a reference? I'm applying for a boson position on the *Gerling,* and Captain Tim is running the show."

"He's a great captain. I loved working under him. Of course. I'll give you my professional contact information later," she said. You'll make a great boson."

"I hope so."

"As soon as we anchor, I want you helping Craig with the slide. Bradley and I will get the rest of the toys in. The cliffs are open, so we can take them over there by tinder. It's going to be hard to entertain these boys."

"I imagine the things we have don't pack the kind of punch they crave. I mean, we do have a governor on the jet skis, so those will be boring as sin."

"They will still have fun on them. Trust me, not everything with these guys has to be a near-death experience. Just watch their alcohol consumption when using the toys. I don't know their team members, and while Reid doesn't usually get drunk, he still likes to have a good time. However, Preston can get pretty nasty when he's wasted, and he doesn't like to be told what he can and can't do."

"It's not like we haven't dealt with that kind of guest before." Kirk nodded. "Can I talk to you about something kind of touchy?"

"Of course. I'm sorry. I didn't realize we weren't done with the serious chat."

"I'm sorry we all put you on the spot in the kitchen earlier. And other times, especially since everything blew up with Kim."

"Don't be. I've been on edge since the whole scene last month, which I should have never put you all in the middle of. I could have handled myself much more professionally."

"For what it's worth, what they did was a shit thing to do, and any of us would have gone off the deep end. We were all just a little blindsided."

"Only thing either one of them did wrong was not tell me before they got involved with each other. But it's all water under the bridge. I'm really fine with them being together." She stared out over the port side of the yacht at the islands and the sun slowly making its descent in the afternoon sky. She'd never tire of being on the water. It would never get old.

Ever.

Especially when her heart and mind were conflicted. It was as if the sky touching the seas below could give her all the answers.

"You know what? I believe you," Kirk said. "There is something different about you today that wasn't there a few days ago. I can't place it, but your confidence and the fierceness in your eyes is at an all-time high. No one can put that there but you. And no one can take that away unless you let them." He patted her shoulder. "I've enjoyed working under you, which is why it was important to me to get a referral from you."

"Why do I sense a *but* coming where I might want to retract my decision?"

"That will be up to you, but I mean it." Kirk leaned back against the railing. "I've had to deal with a couple of female bosons before, and trust me when I say, I've got no issue with women in power. I say bring it on. The more there are, the better off the world would probably be. You've had to fight for every little piece of respect that I get just because I'm swinging a dick. It's not right. It's certainly not fair. I wish I could say I get it, but I don't. I have no idea what it's like to walk in your shoes. However, I will say this." He held up his index and middle fingers. "There are two camps when it comes to how you handle a man's world, and you always seem to choose the harder one."

"Seriously? You want to stand there and tell me that I should use my tits to get what I want in yachting instead of being good at my job *after* you asked me for—"

"I'm not saying any woman should have to do either. That's just a shitty thing all around. I've got five little sisters, and it makes me crazy that they have to deal with things that I don't have to even think twice about. But I digress," Kirk said, letting out a long breath. "You're hands-down the best boson I've ever worked with. I've learned more from you this summer than I have in the last two years I've worked in the yachting industry."

"Thank you for saying that."

"The problem isn't that you come off like a bitch, because you don't. You have a management style that commands respect because you give it in spades. You don't hover over your crew and bark out orders, expecting everyone else to do the heavy lifting; you get right in there, working side by side. But you do it with an attitude that constantly reminds us that the line you draw is a squiggly one, and we're not sure where we stand from one minute to the next."

"What the fuck does that mean?" Of course, she had a good idea if it was anything like Ziggy's explanation for why Darcie didn't make girlfriends.

"Having the gift of sarcasm, a resting bitch face, and a wicked dry sense of humor doesn't give the rest of us a good handle on when you're dicking around. It's why there are so many awkward silences."

Yup. That would be the Ziggy philosophy. Her sister had tried to explain this to her once before but had failed miserably in her description. It was sinking in now.

"So, wait a second," Darcie said. "You're telling me that you guys are confused on when you can make jokes with me and when you can't?"

"And what you might find funny or not." Kirk waved to another deckhand as a larger yacht cruised by.

"I have a sense of humor."

"But it changes. And that's why there is so much tension sometimes with you and the rest of the crew. I'm sure it's the dynamics with Jim, but it's something to consider."

"Other than my catfight with Kim, and the fact that Jim is a womanizing asshole, this is a really good crew."

"None of us can believe she said yes to marrying Jim. No one changes their stripes that quickly."

"When it's the right woman, a man can." She turned and leaned her middle against the railing and stretched out her arms. "Now we just need the music from the movie *Titanic*."

"Are you saying you're a romantic deep down?"

"No. I'm just saying I've known Jim for as long as I've been in this industry. The first time we worked together, I was actually a third stew and he was a first mate."

"You were a stew? Interior? I don't believe it."

"I've done it a couple of times." She tilted her head toward the sun and closed her eyes. "I spent half the season in laundry until one of the deckhands got injured, and Jim suggested they pull me in. I was shocked because we butted heads all the time. Jim and I didn't like each other, but we respected each other." She wrapped her arms around her middle. "I still cringe every time he calls me 'sweetheart' or 'doll' or 'baby.' He just doesn't get it."

"No. He doesn't."

"He's still not the worst man in the world."

"I don't know about that. He cheated on you. That's pretty slimy if you ask me."

Darcie needed to get real with herself about her life and the direction she was headed. It was the only way she'd be able to change course and make it stick. "I was never totally committed to Jim as his girl-friend. While I wasn't at fault for what happened, I had both feet out the door.

"Are you making excuses for him?"

"No. I'm just taking responsibility for my actions and how I ended up where I am today." She blinked her eyes open and inhaled the fresh salty air. Her father had accused her of being lonely.

He also thought she was afraid and that she ran from the things that scared her. He didn't think she was chasing a dream.

He thought she was running from it.

Except, from the time she was a little girl, all she ever dreamed about was the water. The vastness of the ocean. The wide-open space it created. The way the wind raced across the top, making ripples that turned into waves, creating massive swells. It was both life and death.

Whenever she was sad, she used to ride the ferries back and forth between the islands. She would watch the birds dive into the water, looking for fresh fish.

She had nowhere to go and nothing to do. She would just sit and be one with the Sound. The second she stepped off the vessel and headed back to her family, she felt her skin prickle. Her muscles tightened. A thick lump formed in her throat. It made her crazy. She loved her family. She enjoyed every waking moment with them, but the pull to be on the water was too great.

"Um, Darcie. Looks like someone wants to talk to you."

She stepped away from the railing and turned. "Oh. Hey." She stared into Reid's intense blue eyes. They always reminded her of the ocean the first thing in the morning as the sun brought light to the depths below.

"Can I steal you for a few moments?" Reid asked.

"Sure."

"I'm going to go prep the slide," Kirk said. "We're getting close to our anchor spot. I'll make sure everything is ready."

"Thanks." She fiddled with her hair, tightening her ponytail. "Why don't we sit over here?" She glanced toward the bridge, knowing Jim was sitting in his chair, watching her every move. When she dated Jim, for lack of a better word, he'd shown a different side of himself that she wished he'd let the rest of the world see. He could be sweet and charming when he wanted to be, but instead, most saw the arrogant ladies' man who thought he knew everything. "How do you like your accommodations?"

"They're awesome. While stoked they get the master, our youngest team members aren't thrilled they're sharing a bed," Reid laughed. "But Preston and I are too old to share rooms, even if they are twin beds." He rested his arm over the back cushion. He'd changed into a pair of long red boardshorts and a white T-shirt. "It never gets old pulling that kind of shit on the new guys. One of them will either end up on the floor or the sofa, but we're hoping they get drunk enough and don't care so we can sneak in and take pictures."

"Men. You'll get naked with each other. Shower together. But you won't sleep in the same bed."

He leaned a little closer. "Women. You'll sleep in the same bed, but you don't like to get naked with each other. I don't get it."

She shook her head. "Not to mention that's really childish."

"You know what they say about men and boys."

"That I do."

The yacht slowly banked to the right, heading into the cove where it would anchor for the night. She'd been all over the world and had seen some incredibly exotic places, and every single one amazed and touched her soul.

Her back yard was no different.

"I'm glad you came and found me. I wanted to

ask about Deception Pass and what happened to it because it was taken off the activities list and replaced with a scuba diving trip with friends." She raised her hands and made quotation marks with her fingers. "Why would you need your so-called friends to come and get you when we could have tendered you wherever you wanted to go? Within reason. We can also recommend some great places for scuba diving."

"We didn't know our buddies would be here. We just thought it would be fun."

"That's how you're going to play this? Because I know when you're lying to me."

"Fine. Preston blindsided me with Hans, but I'm not fucking around. Hans is a potential business partner. He invited us out on his boat, and he loves scuba diving at night. He's a wannabe extremist and kind of a pain in the ass. However, we couldn't say no without being rude."

"Let me ask you this. Do you want to do business with this Hans guy?"

"Not the point," he said. "But it's one less thing for you to worriy about." He tapped her nose.

She jerked her head back. "Don't do that."

"Sorry. I'm a creature of habit, and I always did that when we were dating."

"Not when I was working, and my boss is glaring at us." She nodded toward the bridge.

"Well, then I should shove my tongue down your throat and stick my hand up your shirt and really give him something to gawk at." Reid tapped his index finger on her knee. "I can't get over the fact you went out with him and that he cheated on you."

"I would have broken up with him at the end of the season, so it doesn't really matter anyway." She tilted her head, wiping the few stray hairs that had blown across her face. "Be honest with me about Deception Pass."

"I am. Although, I'm not the one who got the call. This entire trip is all Preston. If it were up to me, I'd be…nope, I take that back. I like the view where I'm sitting right now."

She tried not to smile, but her mouth denied her mind's wishes.

"Your cheeks are turning pink."

"They are not." If they weren't before, they were flushed now.

"I like how I can still make you blush." He pushed his shades up on top of his head. His blue eyes sparkled in the bright sunshine. "And I wish I could take you in my arms right now and just enjoy this little piece of heaven, but I know that's not possible, and not just because you're working."

She swallowed, her heartbeat.

"Because of the timing of Hans and when he's meeting us, the kayak trip is cancelled and I'm going to need to get at the internet modem by tomorrow morning. Can you make that happen, please?"

"I will let you know for sure at dinner tonight. I'm moving some of my deck crew around on their jobs so I will be on anchor watch."

"I appreciate it."

Her earpiece crackled. "Darcie. Darcie. Captain Jim. Time to drop anchor and then I need you to come to the bridge."

She stood. "Duty calls."

He lifted his thumb and made a gesture over his shoulder. "I guess I should go pretend to have a good time while I try not to stare too hard at you."

"We don't want you to strain your eyes." She patted his chest.

"I'll talk to you later." He turned and strolled toward the stern of the yacht.

He paused. "Do you remember when you were working on that one boat. What was the name? *Rapture?*"

Every inch of her body ignited in flames. She fanned herself. "I do."

"I came to visit, and we stayed in the guest cabin and had some wild sex that night. The cabin was amazing. It was similar to the one I'm in now. It's even on the right side of the vessel."

"It's called the starboard side."

"I'm on the starboard side. Just saying." He winked.

It was only two nights. She could get through two nights without sneaking into his bedroom. Yep.

She could do it.

She had self-control.

She groaned.

CHAPTER 7

*R*eid swirled his whiskey on the rocks, watching the liquid melt the cubes. He loved the way ice rattled inside a glass.

"Can I get you anything else?" Milia asked from behind the bar.

"I'm good, thanks." He'd like a few hours alone with Darcie, but he didn't think that was on the menu.

"Are you going to join the rest of your friends?" She pointed to the hot tub where the boys had ended up. He glanced at his watch. It was close to eight-thirty. "Nah. I'm just going to wait for dinner. I've had enough water for one day." His phone buzzed. He glanced at the screen.

Jagar.

He looked around and decided to take the call on

the top sundeck. He jogged up the stairs, taking them two at a time. He couldn't think of any good reason why Jagar Bowie would randomly call him, even after they'd had a decent conversation. "Hello? Jagar? Is something wrong?"

"I should be asking you that."

"I'm not following."

"Why am I getting anonymous tips that you, and only you, plan on doing some never-done-before stunt off Deception Pass tomorrow night?"

"I don't know. But it's not coming from me."

"Do you remember Matt Montgomery? The guy I was with in New Orleans?"

"The one who hit me, or the one who stuffed his taco in my face?"

"The one with the taco. Why?"

"Just trying to get all the players figured out," Reid said. While the memory was quite painful, he had to admit that it warmed his heart that Darcie had such good friends and family who'd had her back after he broke her heart.

"Well, he's a cop in the city, and he's hearing chatter as well. So I need you to tell me what the fuck is going on."

"Jagar. I don't know."

"Really? Because either you're planning some-thing really fucking stupid that's going to freak my sister out, or you and your little friends are planning something outlandish and trying to throw those of us who might stop it off your trail."

"I'm doing neither. And while I wouldn't put it past Preston to send the press on a wild goose chase, he wouldn't use me to do it. I mean, we've skirted the authorities before. We would know how to do it, and that's not what's going on here."

"I don't believe you."

Reid did a three-sixty, making sure no one was within earshot. "You're going to have to."

"Why? And why are you whispering?" Jagar asked in that overprotective tone.

Reid couldn't blame the man.

"You can't tell anyone this, okay?"

"As long as you're not getting my little sister involved in anything illegal."

Reid pinched his nose. This wasn't going to go over well, but he didn't know what else to do. "I think Preston is trying to push me out of the company. I'm trying to prove it."

"What does that have to do with what I'm hearing?"

"I'm not sure. Every once in a while, a few reporters get bored and like to print bullshit about me or Preston, so it could just be that. But it could also be Preston doing whatever it is he has planned for me. I just don't have a good handle on it, yet."

"How do you know Preston is out to get you?"

"I can't really talk. This might be a superyacht, but it's not that big." He leaned over the side, satisfied that his co-workers weren't concerned with his whereabouts. "I'm hoping to have a better understanding tomorrow when I hack into my company's computer system."

"Why wait?"

"Long story. But your sister is helping me create a ghost WiFi account on the yacht this evening."

"I don't like you bringing her in on this. What does she know, exactly?" Jagar asked.

"More than I want her to, but I did lie to her as much as I could. She and Preston don't like each other as it is, I didn't want tensions running any higher on this vessel than they had to be."

"She hates it when people are dishonest, but I think you did the right thing," Jagar said. "What can I do to help?"

"I wish I knew. I'm flying solo."

"No. You're not. Can you send me an email or text with some details of what you think is going on? I know people. So does my wife. Just make sure whatever you send me isn't illegal. If it even skirts the line of breaking or bending any laws, then we'll have to rethink."

"Why would you help me after everything that happened between me and your sister?"

"Family is everything to me. My sister has spent the last year more lost than she's ever been, and that's because she doesn't have you. And I saw what her not being in your life has done to you when I saw you in New Orleans. The two of you belong together. I know it and I think you do, too."

"I don't know anything right now." His pulse increased when he saw Darcie out of the corner of his eye, headed up the stairs in his direction. "I've got to go. Your sister is about to be in ear shot."

"If you don't let me help, I'll clue her in."

"That's unfair," Reid said.

"You bet. Talk soon."

Reid stuffed his cell into his pocket and took a hefty swig of his whiskey, sucking in one of the ice cubes and crushing it between his teeth.

"Who were you talking to?" She curled her fingers over his biceps and gave his muscle a gentle squeeze. "Did you get news about the person in your office?" she whispered as she peered over the railing.

He should perpetuate the lie. He should keep her in the dark about everything. But when she found out, she'd never want to talk to him again, and that meant he'd have no chance of ever winning her back.

Ever.

"Your brother, Jagar."

"What the fuck? Why?" She took him by the hand and led him down the stairs.

"Where are we going?"

"Shhh."

He followed her all the way to the bow of the boat where they had conversed earlier.

"It's safer to talk up here. No one can really hear us unless they are standing in front of the bridge, and we'd see them." She nodded over her shoulder. "Or walking up the sides, so we just need to keep an eye out."

"Good to know." He took another sip, wetting his whistle. "Is Captain Jim in the cockpit?"

"I'm sure he is," she said, sitting down on the bench. "But I don't care if he sees us."

He joined her, not liking that his back was to the bridge. "What do you think he makes of us being up here together?"

"You and I have a long history. I don't think anyone who knows us would question us having a private conversation. Now, tell me. Why the fuck were you talking to my brother?"

"Maybe we should backtrack to the fact he paid

me a visit this morning."

"You've got to be fucking kidding me. Why would he do that?" She shook her head and picked at her thumbnail.

"Whenever you do that, I want to kiss you, so maybe you shouldn't." He reached out and grabbed her hand. "He's just looking out for his sister. That's all."

"I wish my family would stop fucking meddling in my damned life. It's really starting to piss me off."

He cupped the back of her neck. "I know it feels and looks like meddling. And this morning, I'd agree. He shouldn't have just shown up at my hotel. But I'm in trouble. Big trouble. And he can help. So, I'm sorry. I'll take what you think is meddling but is really just caring about you because Preston is doing some weird shit. And I have to get to the bottom of it." His voice trembled, and his pulse raced out of control. He took in a deep, controlled breath, hoping to keep himself from hyperventilating.

The reality of what Jagar had told him about the rumors smacked his brain like the rain pelting a tin roof. Preston wasn't out to push him out of the company.

No. Preston wanted to publicly ruin Reid, forcing him to leave the company with his tail between his legs.

"Okay. Now you're scaring me."

"I don't mean to, but I lied to you earlier about why I needed to have access to the internet without anyone knowing."

"Lied? How?"

"It's not an employee I'm concerned about. It's Preston." He drew in closer, his lips only inches from hers. He held her gaze, searching for a reason he shouldn't kiss her, other than the fact that she was working, her boss was probably watching, and he knew it would be a mistake.

A big mistake.

For her. She'd be risking her job. Her security. Her heart.

But for him, it would mean the world.

She was his everything, and if he had her on his side, he knew he'd survive Preston and whatever he had planned.

He dropped his hand to his lap and pulled away.

No way would he put her in that kind of position.

"Preston? What is going on with him?" she asked.

"I don't want you to be in the middle of all this. It's bad enough I just roped your brother into it."

"Jagar doesn't get involved in shit unless he wants to be in the thick of it, or unless it's his job," she said. "And as far as I'm concerned. I don't know what's going on, so until you fill me in on the details, I don't get to tell you if I want to be a part of it or not—outside of fucking with the WiFi."

"Right now, that's all I want you to do. I'd never be able to live with myself if anything happened to you."

She took his hand and stood. "We need to get back," she said. "But you have to promise me that you will fill me in as we go. I can't be flying blind. Okay?"

"I can do that. I promise."

"That means if you find anything in the morning when I shut Preston off from the internet, you have to tell me what he's up to, no matter how bad it is."

Reid couldn't take it anymore. He didn't care who was looking. He leaned in and brushed his lips over hers in a sweet, tender kiss. It didn't last very long, but it was the taste of a potential future. "I swear, I will tell you everything. No more lies. No more omitting the truth."

God, he hoped he could keep that promise.

It would be the only way he could have half a chance with Darcie when this was all over.

Of course, they had a shit ton of logistics to work out, but if he had to move to fucking Seattle, he'd do it.

She was worth it.

He should have fought for her to begin with.

* * *

REID SIPPED HIS WHISKEY, watching the moonlight dance on the dark water. A brisk breeze came across the stern. He understood the lure of the seas. He never questioned Darcie's desire to be on it, nor did he want her to give it up.

He just never wanted to be second fiddle. He'd played that role to Erin's depression.

"Why are you looking so glum?" Preston stumbled across the deck and plopped himself down on the lounge chair next to Reid. "We just had one of the best meals of our life, and we're floating on a fucking gorgeous yacht, what is the problem?"

"There isn't one." Reid watched Darcie tie off the tender before she disappeared below deck. He leaned back in his chair and went back to staring at the stars.

"Oh, I know what crawled up your ass now."

Reid chuckled. He absolutely didn't want to hear anything Preston had to say when he got like this. "You've had too much to drink to get all philosophical," Reid said.

"Oh. I'm not doing that. I'm just going to call the

kettle black." Preston waggled his finger. "Darcie has you all fucked up again."

"Not even close," Reid said.

Preston could be a real dick when he was sober, but drunk, he had a real knack for having diarrhea of the mouth and saying shit that just pissed people off. And he knew how to push Reid's buttons, but he didn't usually do it with Darcie. Actually, Preston almost never mentioned her, which Reid thought he did out of respect.

Now, he wondered why Preston did anything, considering he was in the middle of trying to steal the company.

"You can't think straight when she's around. You're useless. And worse, you're souring the mood with our team. They worked hard on this contract and you're being a douchebag."

"I'm just tired. It's been a long day of drinking and being in the sun." He held up his glass. "I'll be more fun tomorrow."

"You're a bad fucking liar." Preston clanked his glass. "She's so far up your ass, she's coming out your mouth. I don't know what you see in her other than she's hot. Does she give good head? Is she a really good fuck? Is that why you can't get over her?"

"Just shut the fuck up. Don't ever talk about her like that again, or I'll beat the shit out of you." Reid glanced over the railing, thankful he didn't see Darcie, though it didn't mean she hadn't heard Preston's hurtful words.

"She's affecting your work."

"Why would you say that now?" Reid asked.

"Seriously? You've done nothing but fuck up since she walked out of your life. Hell. It started the second she came into it. And you've left me holding the bag."

There was no denying Preston was absolutely correct in his observation. But what puzzled Reid was why Preston randomly brought it up on their vacation.

"It's been a year. The time to be concerned about it affecting our business was about nine months ago. But you said nothing. You literally told me to take all the time I needed."

"I wanted to give you some space. You were in pretty bad shape when she dumped you. It looks like you're still not capable of giving me and the company your all."

"It was a mutual breakup," Reid corrected Preston, though he had no idea why he thought that was important. "And you have nothing to worry about when it comes to where my headspace is at."

"You're drooling," Preston said. "You're practically foaming at the mouth, you want her so bad. It's pathetic, and to be frank, man, I don't see what makes her so fucking special that you act like you want to blow your damn brains out. Everyone on the team is commenting on it. They are all worried about you. They have totally seen a change in you just since we walked on this boat. One even asked me if we should be putting away the alcohol."

"Now that's fucking ridiculous. You're the drunk one, and it's clouding your judgment." If only Preston could understand that he was the root cause of Reid's foul mood, not Darcie. If anything, she made the entire situation bearable.

"Not even close," Preston said. "To the judgment part. The drunk part, yeah. I'm there."

"Maybe you should put down both the alcohol and what's coming out of your mouth because you're going to regret this in the morning."

Reid took a swig of his whiskey. He had a decent buzz going, but he'd kept his drinking to a minimum. He wanted to be fresh for when he had access to the WiFi. Of course, he ran the risk that someone at the office would notice him poking around inside the email accounts, contracts that weren't his, and whatever else he could get his hands on.

But it was a risk he had to take.

"I highly doubt that. The only regret I will have is not having the energy to hit on that hot Anastasia.

Damn that chick has an ass. And her tits. I bet those babies are real," Preston said.

"Have you ever loved a woman, Preston? The kind of love that makes your heart beat a little faster and your palms go all sweaty and reminds you of that very first time you realized that feeling was what you lived for?"

"Are you talking about thrill seeking or fucking? Because it sounds like they are one and the same to me."

"Of course you would think that." Reid didn't know why he bothered. Maybe, once they hit dry land, he should just call Preston on his shit and draw the battle lines.

Fuck. He couldn't do that. Not if Preston had gone full-court press already with manufacturing of a product that hadn't been tested and could potentially cause more harm than good if it didn't do what they said it would.

He had to figure this out. Protect himself before departing. There were things in the company that Reid was damn fucking proud of.

And he wanted them.

"You're the expert on love," Preston said. "Did you know Hans didn't randomly call me up last-minute."

Reid's breath caught in his throat. He coughed.

"No. I had no idea."

"This charter is last-minute. I got lucky the boat was available. I paid a pretty penny for it. But the team and I always planned on meeting with Hans. I just wasn't sure if I wanted to include you." Preston let out a short breath that sounded like a slight laugh.

"What does Hans want to do now? Was the jump at Deception Pass supposed to be for him? Were we helping him do something crazy?"

"He nearly peed his pants when he thought his parachute wasn't going to deploy last year. I don't know why he tries all these things. He doesn't have the stomach for it."

"That doesn't answer my question," Reid said.

"Yes. Hans wanted to bungee jump off the bridge. And that still might happen."

"Hans is a wild card, and I don't like the way he does business," Reid said. "He's constantly cutting corners. He had two products recalled last year."

"Neither was his fault," Preston said. "And if you'd ever actually sit down with the man, you might find you'd enjoy doing business with him."

"I doubt that. He's ruthless and not the kind of person who fits into our plan. The only reason we put up with him is the donations he made to our product development."

"Did you ever think that might go away?"

"Sure. But I'm not about to be blackmailed by the likes of Hans Miller. But I guess you are."

"Not even close. But I want you to listen to what Hans has to say. You've blown him off three times over the last few months. That's not good. I need you more present in our business. It's not fair to me or our clients."

"I know I was distracted the first part of this year, but—"

"Distracted? That's a fucking understatement. Until about three months ago, you weren't even present in our business. If you did show up, you were drunk." Preston held up his drink. "Isn't it ironic you're giving me shit now?"

"I know I screwed up. I've apologized, and I'm working my ass off. I don't know what else you want from me. Hell, I didn't even know you felt this resentful toward me." Reid contemplated confronting Preston with his suspicions. Perhaps they could talk it through and work it out, but not when Preston was drunk.

Or this emotional.

And Reid really needed more information because all he really knew was that Preston planned on going behind Reid's back in a business venture with a snake.

"I didn't know either until you started pushing back so hard, and I realized I preferred it when you were off somewhere else licking your wounds," Preston said. "No matter how wild and crazy I get with my need to push the thrill-seeking envelope, I've never left you in a position where you had to deal with everything by yourself."

"That's true. You haven't."

"And then, a couple of months ago, you finally started to get your shit together. You got super excited about the fire suits, which made me want to scream because I could see where that was going."

"If the fire departments—"

Preston held up his hand. "Spare me. I know where you are going. That's the kind of venture that will bury us. But, you have a way of making stuff like that work, and I figured if you did, then I could get you on board with my stuff since the two are so closely related. Or at the very least, keep you occupied so I could seal the deal. But now, you see that little tart, and you're a walking, sulking, heartbroken moron. It's like you can't take a piss without wondering if she'll think it's okay. And now I'm back dealing with a mess of a man who could singlehandedly ruin our company if I turn my back."

"Wow." Reid took a good shot, letting the liquid burn his throat while the words scalded his brain and heart. He set his drink down and flexed his fingers, making sure he didn't make a fist, because he would have a hard time stopping himself from hitting Preston. He wasn't sure where this pent-up resentment had come from, but there was some real venom in that last statement. "I don't even know how to respond to that. I understand I let you down, that I let the people who work for us down, but you said you had it covered. I asked you if you needed me, and you flat out said 'no.'"

"What the hell was I supposed to say? I've been dancing on eggshells for years. It was like I was dealing with my sister," Preston said.

"You did not just fucking say that." Reid clenched his fists. It was rare that Preston poked at Erin's depression, but when he did, he went way low.

"Oh. I did. I've been jumping through hoops trying to keep you happy. During the negotiations with the production company, I thought you were finally back. I mean, the guy I knew before my sister and then this Darcie chick fucked him all up."

"What the hell does that mean?"

"My sister softened you. She made you weak. Once she died, it was like she sucked the extremist right out of you. I'd see sparks of it here and there and I'd try to feed the beast, but nothing. Then fucking Darcie. Oh. My God. It was like watching the worst romantic mush you could find on those stupid cable channels. I wanted to slit my throat watching the two of you fall in love. Only it went bad. And quick. And last night, she walked by, and everything changed. I don't get the hold she has over you, and why you can't shake it and get back to what's important."

"I think you're the one who's lost track of why we started all this," Reid said, having a little better understanding of what drove Preston, but no clue how to deal with it all. "Darcie doesn't have any control over me. It's just weird to see her again, that's all." *Weird* wasn't even close to the right word. More like intense. Surreal.

Perfection.

"Do you remember Erin's memorial?" Preston asked out of the blue.

"What the hell kind of question is that?" Reid glared. When Erin died, he'd lost more than the woman he loved, he also lost Preston. It took Reid until this year to figure that out, but her death had put a wedge between them so deep that it could never be removed. Preston saw his sister as baggage.

Her depression.

Her mental illness.

Those were things he couldn't tolerate. They

needed to be hidden. Brushed under the rug, never to be seen by anyone.

He wanted to pretend that it didn't exist.

It was part of the reason he'd never wanted Reid to become romantically involved with Erin in the first place, but Preston couldn't ever voice it out loud.

"Of course I do, but why are you bringing it up now?"

"You loved my sister."

"I did," Reid said. Tears burned the corners of his eyes. A day didn't pass where he didn't have at least one thought of Erin. Their relationship hadn't been very long, only about a year, but it had been passionate, and she'd taught him what love was all about.

She also showed him that loving someone sometimes meant letting them go, and that's what her last words had been to him. He hadn't known at the time that she planned on taking her life, making it look like an accident, in a bid to spare his.

To this day, that concept gave him goosebumps.

"I've never understood why. I mean, I get why she fell for you, but never got what you saw in her," Preston said.

"You're an asshole."

"I know," Preston said. "But I'm not sure I believe you."

"What the fuck does that mean?"

"If you loved my sister as much as you say you did, you'd be doing what you promised her when you helped spread her ashes over East Buffalo Peak." Preston stood and hovered over Reid. "Do you remember what that was?"

Reid nodded. His insides trembled, and his chest hurt when he tried to take in a deep breath.

"The fire-retardant line is something my sister would want us to press hard with, and not just with the fire departments. That's the no-brainer. Of course she'd want that. But you know how she felt about safety for the masses."

"I think you're missing the point in what your sister wanted."

"If she could save the life of a man running from a burning building, she'd do it." Preston wiped his upper lip and let out a short breath. "Hans wants to partner with us. He knows we have a fire suit that withstands temperatures hotter than anything else on the market. He also knows we've been working on technology to reduce the weight and weave it into fabric."

"Why the fuck would you tell him that?" Reid jumped to his feet, knocking over the table that held his drink. The glass shattered on the fiberglass floor. "That technology hasn't been tested for that use, much less even brought down to that level. We have no idea how it will work or if it will be approved. You promised me we'd do this right."

One of the girls on the interior crew made a comment and came running, but Reid ignored her and kept his focus on Preston.

"I promised after the fact. And frankly, I lied," Preston said. "Hans would be a good partner. He can do things we can't."

"What have you done?" Reid asked. "Have you already cut a deal with Hans?"

"Excuse me," Milia said quietly as she cleaned up the broken glass and scurried off inside the main cabin.

"That's what this meeting is all about."

"Cancel the fucking meeting."

"Not on your life. I'm doing what is necessary," Preston said, giving Reid a little poke in the chest. "And you need to get your fucking head in the game and start honoring my sister and what you promised her. This would have been the project she got on board with, and you know it."

"You're really going to use your dead sister to manipulate me to do what you want?" Reid swallowed the bile rising in the back of his throat. Preston could be shallow and self-absorbed. In business, everyone would describe him as ruthless but brilliant.

However, Reid never expected that Preston would blatantly stoop so low.

But he should have known.

"I'm simply reminding you of a promise you made to the person you once told was the only woman in the world, at least for you." Preston ran his hand through his blond hair. "Or did you forget you professed such a profound love, and said that you'd always honor her wish, no matter what happened?"

"You're fucking drunk." Reid took a step forward. "If Erin were alive and listening to you she'd—"

"Don't you dare lecture me on what my sister would do if she were here." Preston stood two inches away. He puffed out his chest and narrowed his stare. "Now, do what you promised Erin before and after she died."

"Good evening, gentlemen." Captain Jim strolled through the doors to the outer deck. "Is everything okay out here?"

"I was just heading inside to get myself another drink." Preston took his glass and downed the last gulp. "You have an amazing chef. Dinner was fantastic. See you in the morning."

Reid turned and gripped the railing. A water taxi

cut through the channel as it went from yacht to port. Reid took in a few deep, cleansing breaths. Preston hadn't been wrong, and he had every right to be pissed as hell. But to use Erin's death...that was a new low, even for Preston.

Something else was going on, and it made Reid wonder if there were other problems in the company.

All the more reason to get a better look without Preston knowing what he was doing. Maybe he should do that tonight. The boys were all drunk enough. No way would they be logging into anything.

Except for the alerts.

He needed to deal with the those, and that would be complicated.

"My chief stew said things were getting a little heated," Jim said. He leaned against the railing about two feet away. "Do I need to have someone cut him off?"

"He'll pass out soon enough."

"Half of your team has turned in."

"The two who are still up are just waiting for Preston to say he's had enough. He knows how to party, but he's not usually this bad. I apologize for his angst."

"We've had worse, trust me."

"I've heard stories from Darcie." Reid turned and folded his arms across his chest, but he made sure he kept Preston in his peripheral vision. No way would he let that man out of his sight until he went to bed. "She told me what you did, and for the record, I think you're an asshole for it."

Jim ran a hand across his face. "You're the jerk who let her get away."

"I guess I am."

"She and I never would have worked. We both had one foot out the door," Jim said.

"She's good at that."

"I know," Jim said. "She's not very good at commitment. Nor was I. But you and she, you two belong together. It's obvious."

"That's funny, coming from you." Reid wasn't about to argue the point because in part, he agreed. He just wasn't sure how to make it happen.

"If you need anything at all, just let me know." Jim strolled back into the main cabin.

Reid pulled out his cell phone. Time to take a big risk.

CHAPTER 8

*D*arcie finished hosing down the lower aft deck. She glanced at her watch and yawned. Preston and his young team knew how to party, and someone had to stay up until the last of the guests was asleep. Tonight it was her, Kirk, and Milia.

"Everything is cleaned up by the hot tub," Kirk said. "Milia is just finishing up in the galley."

"You can go to bed," she said.

"Thanks. What time do you want me on in the morning?"

"Take the last shift."

Kirk nodded, taking the hose from her hands. "Only if you let me finish up here."

"Fair enough." She headed down toward her cabin she shared with Milia now that Kim had left the ship, only Darcie didn't want to go there. She stopped at the crew mess for a quick snack. She pulled open every cabinet three times, and the only thing that was even remotely appealing was the bag of Oreo cookies.

Well, that would go right to her hips.

Who cared? She pulled them from the cabinet and ripped them open just as Milia appeared. "Preston finally went to bed."

"He was pretty hammered."

"I bet he sleeps until noon." Milia pulled out the milk and poured two glasses.

Having girl-bonding time was the last thing Darcie wanted. "Preston might be a nasty drunk, but he bounces back quickly."

"He and Reid were going at it pretty good after dinner. Something about a girl. Erin?"

"I heard part of it." Darcie didn't want to gossip about Reid's past, or his late girlfriend, with the chief stew. "It's best to just leave that one alone."

Holding her phone up, she found the text thread with Jagar. "I'm sorry. I need to talk with my brother."

"No worries. I'll just take these to our room. See you in a bit." Milia snagged a few more treats and scurried off down the tight hallway.

Darcie hadn't been lying when she said she

needed to have a chat with her brother, but she just didn't want to listen to Milia anymore.

Darcie: Why did you visit Reid this morning?

Might as well go right for the jugular—no need to beat around the bush.

Jagar: Because my wife told me I should.

Darcie: Really? You're going to toss Callie under the bus?

Jagar: Are you going to yell at a pregnant lady?

Darcie: Tell me what's really going on. And for the record. I know Preston is coming for him. He told me. I can also see how scared he is, I just don't know what he's really afraid of or what he's really doing about it.

Jagar: I don't either. He just emailed me some information that I'm sharing with Matt and Asher. I'm working on it. I promise you.

Darcie: What do I need to do?

Jagar: Just keep an eye out and do your job. Let me do mine.

Darcie: Why do I get the impression that you know more than I do?

Jagar: Because I do. And I can't tell you what I know.

Darcie: Why not?

Jagar: Two reasons. One of them is I'm putting myself in a bad spot, so I'm protecting myself. The second reason is I'm protecting you.

Darcie had had enough of texting. She hit the call

button.

Jagar picked up on the first ring. "I wondered how long that would take."

"You know how much I hate it when you of all people pull that shit, shielding me from the big bad world. I'm a grown-up. I don't need my big brother deciding what—"

"I'm safeguarding you from being involved in something illegal, okay?"

"Don't fuck with me, Jagar." She took a cookie and dunked it into her milk and then stuffed the whole thing into her mouth. The white liquid dribbled down her chin. She chewed and chewed, trying not to choke. "Why would I be breaking the law?"

"We can't talk about this. You just have to trust me."

"I still love him," she whispered.

"I know."

"I don't want to. I've tried not to."

"I know how impossible that is to do," Jagar said.

"He's different."

"So are you."

"I'm worried about whatever is going on with him and Preston. You have to tell me."

"I can't, and I won't. Not yet anyway."

"If you won't, I'll go to the source." She didn't give her brother a chance to argue or even say goodbye.

She tapped the red button on the screen and tucked her cell into her pocket, leaving the milk and cookies behind.

On her tiptoes, she made her way to the guest cabins and found the one on the starboard side. She raised her hand to knock, but the door opened.

Reid stretched out his arm and yanked her into the room. "What the hell do you think you're doing?"

She fell back onto the bed and blinked. "You told me to come for a visit." She bent her knees up and rested her head in the palm of her hand, smiling seductively.

"Jagar just called me. You did not come here for a booty call."

"Maybe my brother shouldn't tell me that one of you might be doing something illegal."

"Fuck." He held up the phone and tapped the screen. "Your brother is on speaker. What the hell did you tell her?"

"Enough to get her into your room because this is bullshit," Jagar said. "The only way this works is if she knows because we can't bring Jim in on it."

"Why not?" Reid sat down on the edge of the bed. "An hour ago, you agreed Jim would be the best bet."

"Nope. He's a fucking big risk, that's what he is," Jagar said.

"Wait a second." Darcie ran her hand through her

157

hair, finding a decent strand and twisting it between her fingers. She shifted, tucking a foot under her butt. "You two have been conspiring and not talking to me?"

"I wouldn't go that far," Reid said. "But Preston and I had words after dinner, so I needed to get into the system."

"We have your ghost or whatever internet connection all set up."

"That's only part of the problem and all that really does is allow me to work without Preston, or anyone on this ship, know that I'm doing it because no one can see that connection but me. However, I've been so out of touch with the company, I don't know who I can trust. And if I were to start looking at emails, even ones that are left on the server that I have access to, Preston would be notified. And then I figured he would know that I was on to him."

"That's when I remembered that our cousin Sally just got a job working—"

Darcie interrupted her brother. "Sally's a hacker."

"She's an ethical hacker," Jagar said.

"And I hired her to do a sweep of the system by seeing how easy it would be to hack into it and get rid of the warnings," Reid said.

"That's sneaky," Darcie said, totally impressed, which she shouldn't be. "What did you find out?"

"Sally is getting all that information to Reid. I will only get involved if necessary," Jagar said. "And I didn't want you involved. I shouldn't even be this close at this point. While there isn't anything illegal about what Reid has done so far, I'm about to do something that is crossing a line."

"Don't do it if you're not comfortable." Reid took her hand, pressing his lips to her skin. "You've done more than enough."

"Well, there was one thing that came up when Sally first got into the system that got her attention and got her flagging me. It was an email address for one of the anonymous tips about you jumping off Deception Pass."

"Did it come from my company?" Reid asked.

"No. But someone is communicating with Preston. Sally didn't mean to read the email, but once she did, she had to send it to me. Now, I'm stuck between a rock and a hard place."

"What did the email say?" Darcie asked. "And who was it from?"

"It says: *I agree with the new plan. I've already sent out the rumors. It won't matter how it happens, we will be able to create enough speculation that we'll be covered.* And it was sent from *The Weatherby*."

Darcie jumped to her feet. "What?"

"Someone on that yacht is communicating with

the ouside world and setting this up. And from what little detective work I've done so far," Jagar said, "all fingers point to Jim."

* * *

REID REACHED out and curled his fingers around Darcie's forearms. "Stop pacing." When she got angry, she was like a raging inferno blazing out of control with no water source in sight.

"How the hell can you be so calm?" she asked.

"Trust me, I'm not. But until I sort through all the information that your cousin was able to get me, and we figure out if Jim is actually part of this conspiracy, there isn't much we can do."

"How could you go to my brother behind my back?"

"I didn't," Reid said. "I haven't seen you to tell you what I did."

"Would you have told me?"

"I don't know." Reid let out a long breath. "If I had found out about Captain Jim before you, I might have kept that to myself until this was over."

"At least you're being honest."

He cupped her cheeks. "I don't want you in the middle of this. I'm shocked your brother sent you here knowing Jim might be involved. And I'm beginning to think Preston is dangerous. I mean, deadly dangerous. And that scares me."

"Did you ever think I might be able to help, and Jagar knows it?" she said with an arched brow and the corner of her mouth tipped upward.

"That doesn't mean any of you need to put your careers on—"

"Would you just shut up?" She raised up on tiptoe and pressed her mouth to Reid's lips. It wasn't a long kiss, or a passionate one.

But it was a powerful one, and it told him that he'd better listen to the woman in his arms or else he might not get a second chance.

Ever.

"I want to see that email that Jim supposedly sent." She held onto his wrists. "I know his personal email. I also know how he writes. Actually, I want to see every email that you have from that address."

"I don't think that's a good idea," Reid said.

"Why not? And if you say you're trying to protect me, I'll knee you."

He cringed. "Is it so bad to want to make sure nothing bad happens to you?"

"No. I think it's sweet. But it doesn't change anything. Now, I'll go get my computer."

"No need." He'd lost his fucking mind. He should be telling her to go back to her cabin and let him

deal with his problems. Only Jagar, for some godforsaken reason, had pushed her right into the fire. "I've
got a tablet that will let you look at everything."

"Everything?" she asked.

"Yes. You might as well help me sort all the data."

"That sounds really fucking boring," she said.
"How does a thrill seeker cope with that?"

"It's rough. But we manage." He handed her his
tablet. "And it will probably take all night. I haven't
paid much attention to the business since we broke
up. The last two months, I wrapped up a deal with a
thrill-seeking company in Colorado. Preston
thought it would be good for me to focus on one
small project while I got my shit together, and I
agreed."

She fluffed the pillow and sat cross-legged on the
bed with the tablet resting on her bare thighs.

He groaned. Deciding he needed to keep a little
distance, he set up his computer at the desk.

"Oh no," she mumbled.

"What is it?"

She tapped the screen. "That's an email Jim uses
for personal use. He's got a few of them."

"Are you sure? Does he use it to communicate
with you?"

She shook her head. "It's his Netflix and Hulu
email."

"Text your brother and tell him you think it's him. If he got more than one anonymous tip about me from that email, maybe he can use that to prove it belongs to Jim."

"All right," she said. "Random question, but did Preston pick the project in Colorado, or did you?"

"He did, but I was happy to do it. I knew the people that owned the company, and the travel back and forth wasn't too bad." He pulled up the mirror server. Sally was still populating all the work emails. If anyone had anything personal, well then, too bad for them. If anyone had sent anything and deleted it, a copy would be kept for six months. All contracts that had not expired would be in the proper folders. Ones that had not been executed could be anywhere, knowing Preston.

Reid would focus only on Hans, manufacturing, and the fire suit. He'd also have to look for any patents that were pending and a few other things, but that would take longer than all night.

"You didn't find it strange that he put you on a project that required you to go to where Erin died."

His fingers hovered over the keyboard. His jaw slackened. "I hadn't thought about it."

"I heard what he said to you earlier, and for the record, it was a shitty thing to say."

"I thought so, too." Reid turned. "But I'm used to

that from Preston, especially when he gets drunk and starts going off about Erin. It's his way of coping. He did lose his sister, and he is hurting, too. And don't take this the wrong way, but I think you being here is a reminder she's not."

"I don't take offense to that," Darcie said as her fingers pressed the screen.

"You were right about how I used Erin as an emotional shield when things got a little too heavy with us, and I got scared. In the beginning."

"I'm the one who put Erin between us," Darcie said.

"You did like to bring her up at the weirdest times. Why would you do that?"

"Because I wanted to understand you better. You could be so intense at times, and she obviously meant the world to you. But you and Preston never talked about her, and I thought that was weird."

"Preston and I do have an oddball dynamic."

"That part of the relationship was way past being quirky," Darcie said. "You loved Erin."

Reid tapped his chest. "I did. I do."

"He was your best friend, and yet the two of you can't share the one thing that bonds you together in the tightest of ways. That always frightened me."

"Why?"

"Have you met my family?" she asked with a

raised brow. "You can't be an outsider when you date a Bowie. That's only reserved for the baby of the family."

"Stop. You're not an outsider in your family." He snagged a piece of paper and tossed it. She had this horrible habit of withdrawing from her family. The first time he'd seen her do it, he'd worried that Darcie might have some of the same problems Erin had. But over time, he learned that Darcie's only issue was that she was too hard on herself and took everything everyone said to heart. "Why do you always have to do that?"

"I don't know. Probably because I'm avoiding them. However, we're not talking about me. We're talking about you and Preston and how you never talked about Erin, and that bothered me. Did it bother Preston? Her family?" Darcie set the tablet aside and sat up a little taller, twirling her hair around her finger.

"No. They're the ones that refused to discuss her, and I had to learn to live with the fact that I couldn't save her. No one could, and that was a demon I didn't know how to live with. I used to feel guilty about loving you, as if I shouldn't. And when we got serious, I got scared because I started to want all those things I told myself I'd never have after Erin died. It freaked me out a bit, and now that I've had some time to reflect, I can see how I made you feel as if you were in her shadow."

"You never made me feel that way. I said that because I wanted to hurt you and because Preston put in my head," she said. "There's something I never told you about Preston from when we were dating." She plopped her thumb between her teeth and chewed on her nail.

"I don't like the sound of that." He wadded up another piece of paper. This time it landed right on her nose. He winked.

"He told me about Erin before you did. And he told me about how you blamed yourself for her death."

"I did torture myself with that for a long time. But as I told you, Erin was bipolar and suffered from severe depression. She tried to cover it, and when she was younger, she did so pretty well. But near the end, she was just all over the place."

"Preston would tell me when the two of you would go on some of your thrill-seeking adventures that you would go off by yourself and sometimes carry off some crazy stunt. He showed me videos of you doing some stupid things."

Reid laughed. "I'm sure those images were from when I was young, like in my early twenties. Maybe from even before I met him and Erin."

"Maybe. But he said you were the one with the death wish, not him. He made himself out to be the one who always had to keep you in check."

"That's funny because I'm a safety nut with a checklist."

"But I believed him at first."

"I don't find that amusing at all," he said, glancing at the screen. Sixty-eight percent left to go.

"Preston would tell me he often worried because you always said it should have been you and not Erin who died. But he told me that sometimes you'd get really drunk and say how you wished you could join her."

"I think that's pretty normal, and I probably said that in the first month or two after she passed, but I didn't say it regularly." He leaned forward and rested his elbows on his knees. "Why are we talking about this?"

"Preston told me you'd never be able to get over Erin's death. That if I looked close enough, you had constant reminders of her everywhere."

"I didn't realize you and Preston spent that much time together." Fuck. He did have reminders of Erin all over his world. They had a product named *The Erin*. And out of respect for her family, who he saw often, he had pictures of her in his house. He did nothing to erase her from his life.

"We didn't. He would whisper these little jabs in my ear when we were together, or I'd get a text occasionally."

"Why didn't you ever tell me?"

"I wanted to believe that Preston was just heartbroken about his sister. I know how I would feel if I lost one of my siblings. Just thinking about it makes my eyes burn." She lifted her shirt, unfortunately—or fortunately—showing off a black lacy bra and dabbed above her cheeks. "By the time we were at the end of our relationship, Preston had me believing I was just a fill-in for his sister."

"Oh, Darcie." He pushed his chair back and sprawled out on the bed. "Erin was the first woman I ever loved, but I never meant for her to be a comparison stick for you and me. I'm sorry that you were made to feel that way. I can't believe Preston did that to you, especially when he knows why I kept all those keepsakes of Erin."

"Why did you?"

"Because of how she died. I needed to remember the two sides of Erin. I believe it's important, and I know she never wanted me to forget the complicated parts of her. She and I talked about her illness. About her depression. But she lied to me and to herself." Reid wiped a tear that rolled down the side of his face. "In the end, I thought she had it under control, but I listened to Preston. To his family. I didn't listen to my heart. To what my soul told me was true, and that was that Erin was in trouble."

"Do you know that I've never seen Preston use any emotion when he speaks of his sister?"

"They really weren't close."

"Was that because he was ashamed of her mental illness?"

"Her entire family was. They still are. I'd never experienced anyone with that kind of depression before. I didn't understand it or the emotional rollercoaster she put me on, and I had no one to talk to. Preston wouldn't listen. Her parents just thought she was moody. When she died, I felt like I had failed her because I did what everyone else had done in her life and pretended she wasn't suicidal."

"She never told you she wanted to die, did she?"

Reid shook his head. "She told me all the time, but I thought because she either failed at doing it before I met her, or because she hadn't tried when we were dating that it was just her illness. But deep down I knew how badly she wanted the pain to end. And to this day, her family still won't acknowledge what she did or how she felt. And Preston destroyed the proof."

"What proof?" She set the tablet on the nightstand and rolled to her side. "There's proof that Erin killed herself? You never told me she left a note."

"She kept a journal, and she wrote her thoughts in it. Preston got rid of it."

"How do you know? What did he do with it?"

"It was on her computer. I read about a month's worth of her ramblings. It nearly killed me that I'd had no idea what kind of suffering she was going through every day and how hard she tried to be happy, for me. She wanted so much to be *normal* for me. She thought killing herself would give me a chance at having the kind of life I deserved." He ran his thumb over Darcie's cheek, his skin dampened from her tears.

"I'm so sorry for the things I said about your feelings for Erin."

"Don't be." He brushed his lips over her forehead. "When you and I first hooked up, I did use Erin as a way to protect myself. I did it with all women because I never wanted to hurt that bad again. But as time went on, and I fell in love with you, I realized that the biggest reason I didn't let go of Erin wasn't because of guilt, it was because she gave me strength. Erin was a special woman, and I'll always want to honor her life, just not in the way Preston wants me to." He squeezed his eyes shut. "He's using my love and grief for his sister to manipulate me."

"He's been doing that for ten years. I'm sorry. I've seen it and I should have said something."

Reid blinked. His heart beat so fast, he thought it might jump right out of his chest. "When you came into the picture, I stopped letting him manipulate me as much. Then I went crazy when we broke up and I did leave him holding the bag."

"So that gives him the right to push you out of your own company?" She wrapped her arm around his middle and slipped her knee between his legs. Her petite yet firm body molded to his like a pair of leather driving gloves.

"Of course not. But he lost his sister. They might not have been as close as you and your siblings, but her death still changed him fundamentally. And weirdly, I suppose he blames me or some weird shit. I don't know. I'm just trying to figure what and why."

"But you're not responsible for him, which is what you've been doing ever since she died. You've made excuses for him and all but catered to his every whim."

"Until I fell in love with you," Reid said. "And since then, he's been working on getting rid of me."

"I didn't like him when we were dating. I dislike him even more now."

He pulled her tight to his chest, running his hands up and down her back. It had been so long since he'd held her, and it felt as though he'd come home. "I never understood why he didn't want us together, other than I believe he saw the writing on the wall."

"And what writing was that?"

"I wanted to take the company in a different direction."

"Like how?"

"I love developing products that will keep people safe. This fire suit we're working on could really change things for firefighters across the nation. I want to focus on partnerships like that. But it takes time, patience, and money. Preston wants to focus on the extreme sports like the stunt movies, but he's always cutting corners, and I'm afraid it will end up costing lives just to make a few million when he's already got plenty of money. When is enough enough?"

"Ten million? Twenty?"

He cocked his head back.

She shrugged. "Sorry. It's very different when you're below deck and have always had to work for a living. And I'm not judging the fact that you were born with money. It's not like my family was poor, but what you're going to give us for a tip was the down payment for my sailboat."

"It's not about the money anymore for me. Nor is

it about the thrill. It is about honoring Erin in a way and doing something good with what used to be my stupidity."

Darcie pressed her hand to the center of his chest and smiled. "Being in your cabin right now is about one of the dumbest things I've ever done. Milia is probably sneaking around the boat, wondering where I am, and that might give this crew something to talk about."

"I think they already are. And I've seen the cabins you have to sleep in. I'd be claustrophobic, not to mention the shower and toilet being in the same space. I don't know how you do it."

"This coming from a man who has slept on the side of a cliff for shits and giggles." She kissed his neck. "Our lifestyles aren't all that different when you think about them. We are both motivated by the need to feel something flow through our bodies. Yet we don't ever really allow ourselves to feel what is important."

"I feel everything when I'm with you." He inhaled the sweet scent of her vanilla and strawberry shampoo. He missed the long, leisurely nights he'd spent with her in his arms as they stared at the stars and listened to the night sounds. When he met her, it'd been a time in his life where he'd been coming out of a fog, figuring out who he really was and what he wanted. He'd wandered through his adolescence with no real guidance from his parents. He'd been a rich kid with a credit card. Thankfully, he had a nanny with a conscience.

He kissed Darcie's cheek. Her temple. And then moved to her plump, adorable lips that tasted like bananas and peaches.

"We should probably start looking at the emails and stuff," he whispered.

"Do you think it's all downloaded by now?" she asked as she pressed her breasts against him, raising her leg just a little higher.

He reached over her and snagged the tablet. "Eighty-six percent done, so we have maybe a half-hour."

She lifted her shirt over her head and tossed it to the side. It landed on his laptop, shifting it, closing the lid. "Oops," she said, straddling him. "That gives us just enough time."

"Considering the last time I had sex with a woman was with you, we might be lucky if I last an eighth of that time." He gripped her hips, holding her steady. He truly was terrified that it might be over before he even got out of the gate. He groaned when she bit down on her lower lip.

"You're joking," she said.

"Nope."

"So, either I need to take your instant reaction as you're really happy to see me, or you're just happy to see anyone."

He reached up and quickly unclasped her bra, letting the straps roll off her sexy shoulders. He traced a path over her small, perky breast. He palmed them both before flicking her nipples, making them tighten and pucker.

She arched her back, rolling her hips a little to the left and then a little to the right.

His toes curled, and he did his best to ignore the pleasure she brought him and focus instead on the hard nubs under his fingers. He raised up and held one nipple close to his mouth. He licked his lips, letting the tip of his tongue gently stroke across her soft skin.

She took a long breath, lifting her boob closer to his mouth.

He teased her again, this time with his teeth, barely touching her.

"Do I need to feed it to you?" She grabbed his face. Her breath came in short, choppy pants.

He glanced between her hot gaze and her hard nipple. He pinched it before sucking it into his mouth. Wrapping his arms around her waist, he rolled her to her back and settled between her legs, switching from one tantalizing nipple to the other, making sure they were both properly assaulted.

She tugged and yanked at his shirt.

Reluctantly, he rocked back on his knees, ditching his top. "Whoa." He looked down as she planted her warm lips on his stomach.

Her fingertips dipped inside his shorts.

For two seconds, he thought about stopping her, but then she blinked, staring up at him with her mesmerizing blue eyes that held him captive.

She could be torturing him right now and he wouldn't care.

He swallowed.

Hard.

Standing at the edge of the bed, his fingers in her hair, watching her touch him in ways he'd thought would never happen again, he realized he'd never be able to let her go.

It would kill him.

"Come here."

She kissed her way up his stomach, over his chest, and to his mouth. His tongue greeted hers with a fiery passion. Quickly, he removed the rest of her clothing and shoved her back onto the bed.

A little too harshly as she banged the headboard.

She laughed. "My turn, cowboy." She sucked on her index finger before gliding it across her opening, dipping it inside and then bringing it back to her mouth. "Mmmm."

"I could just stand here and watch." He grabbed himself and stroked once.

"We've tried that before. You can't handle it." Her pink tongue glided up her middle finger and then down her index finger. She took both and shoved them inside herself, sliding in and out while her other hand pinched her nipple and she smiled wickedly. Her chest heaved up and down, and her breathing became erratic.

He let go of himself and crawled on the bed. "You're right. I can't handle it, and it takes you longer."

"We don't know that."

He chuckled. "I bet I can make you come in less than three minutes."

"I'd kind of like it to last a little longer than that."

He took her hand and sucked on her fingers. "Don't worry. I'll make sure it happens at least one more time."

"You better."

While their relationship had been riddled with misunderstandings, arguments, and meddling from others, they had always been perfect in intimate moments.

And not just sex, though he had never had any

complaints in that department.

He slipped his fingers inside and ran his tongue over her hard nub. She tasted like sweet nectarines with a touch of honey. He found the spot that made her hips sink into the mattress.

She dug her fingers into his shoulders. "Oh God, yes."

Holding her stomach, he continued swirling his tongue, nibbling with his teeth each time she moaned, timing it with the rolling of her hips.

Her belly quivered. Her knees slammed into the sides of his face. "Oh. My. God."

He loved the way her body moved as it convulsed with pleasure.

"Kiss me," she whispered.

"Gladly."

She arched, accepting him inside. "I've missed you." She wrapped her arms and legs around him, digging her heels into the backs of his thighs. Their tongues followed the same rhythm as the rest of their motions.

"Yes. Yes," she whispered, grinding her hips. "Please. Now."

He growled, slipping his hand between their bodies and finding the spot that would send her over the edge. He rubbed gently, flicking his finger left and right moving in a small circle while trying desperately not to let his climax explode before her second one coated him.

He held his lower body as still as he could, but she wiggled her hips, shimmying this way and that way. He wasn't sure if it was to help his hand or if she wanted him deeper inside, but she was about to get both. Breaking off the kiss, he raised his chest, giving himself a little more room to work his magic. He pressed his lips over her nipple.

"Oh, Reid. Yes."

He pumped, losing all control as his climax merged with hers in a powerful expulsion. All he could think about was that he had to have broken the condom.

Only he wasn't wearing one.

He collapsed to the side, holding her tightly as he worked to catch his breath.

His computer dinged.

"I think the download is done," he said.

"Perfect timing."

He chuckled, taking her chin with his thumb and index finger. "How's the timing with birth control?"

"What do you mean?"

"We didn't use protection."

"Oh, shit. I'm not currently taking any birth control, and I would say our timing might be a little too skewed in the wrong direction."

"Well, nothing we can do about it now. We'll just have to wait it out." He kissed her forehead. "Are you still against having children?"

"I never said I didn't want them. I just said I didn't see how they fit in my life."

"And now?"

"I'm not against them." She rolled to her stomach. "I'm struggling with what I want to do with my life. I'm taking my captain's test, and I want to captain a superyacht at least once in my life, but I don't know if I want to be forty years old and catering to a bunch of rich drunks while babysitting immature idiots."

"Yeah. That doesn't sound all that appealing. But what would you do if you didn't captain a superyacht?"

"I had planned on taking the time on this charter to evaluate my career choices, but I've been distracted."

"I know that feeling," he said. "But if you had to make a decision right this second, what would it be?"

"Well. If I got to captain for say a year, I think maybe teaching. I was offered a position managing the marina and running the sailing school. I could see myself doing something like that in a few years."

"Looks like you have a plan."

CHAPTER 9

*D*arcie arched her back and twisted left and right. Her cell showed three-thirty in the morning. They'd been at this for a few hours, and she wasn't sure if she was going down the wrong road, but as she arranged the cryptic conversations and the dates they had been exchanged, a thought formed in her head and it pissed her right the fuck off. "I found something disturbing in these emails with Jim."

"What's that?" Reid stood behind her and dug his finger into her shoulders and neck, massaging gently, but firmly.

She dropped her head and closed her eyes for a long moment, letting the tension ease out of her muscles. Being with Reid again only added to her confusion on what to do with her life. She had no life skills outside of yachting. Perhaps her father might have had a point about college and having a backup plan, but she wasn't about to tell him that.

Though the more she thought about teaching, the more she liked it.

But she would give being captain a good year.

Maybe two.

Depending on the boats and the crew. But she knew beyond that, her career path needed a shakeup.

"The very first one I found is dated six months ago. Based on the language, it seems obvious they had prior communication, but perhaps not through this email. Anyway, the email reads: *She's agreed.*"

"That's it? And that's from Jim?"

"Yes. But what I find interesting is that is right around the time Jim called me out of the blue and asked me to come work for him."

"So, you think him saying *she's agreed* is him referencing you?"

She pulled up a couple of the emails and pointed to the screen. "All of these coincide with my time-lines for the two vessels I've been on with Jim since you and I broke up. In this one, Jim tells Preston that she's right where they want her. And in this one, which is dated two months ago, Jim tells Preston not to worry, that he's already cleared the surprise charter, and Preston responded back with, and I quote: *Good. This will be fun to see how it all plays out and which story will end up being printed.*"

"That's weird."

She lifted her gaze. "They've also been planning this for months. As in, Jim used me right from the get-go. I was always part of whatever this plan is."

The rosy color in Reid's cheeks drained as his jaw slackened.

"Us meeting wasn't a chance encounter," she said.

"They've been playing us from day one, and it's not just me he's going to destroy. He's going to get you, too," Reid said. "I'm going to fucking kill both of them." He took two large steps toward the door.

"Fuck. No." She bolted from the chair and charged to the front of the cabin. She flattened her back against the wood.

"Get out of my way."

"I will not," she said. "Confronting them now isn't going to help us, especially out here at sea. If Preston doesn't know we have any of this information, it will give us some time to form a plan. Besides, if we can find anything illegal in these documents, my brother, Matt, and Asher will be all over that shit."

"You expect me to just sit out there, drink beer, ride jet skis and pretend like I don't know any of this? I'm not that good of an actor."

"You're going to have to be."

"Fucking-A." He smashed his fist into his hand. "Someone needs to tell that fiancée of Jim's that she's marrying a dirtbag."

"Don't worry. I will. As a matter of fact, when this is all over, I'm going to enjoy having Jim fired." Darcie arched a brow. "Can I trust you not to leave this room if I step away from the door?"

"I'll only make that promise if I get a kiss."

She rose on tiptoe and brushed her lips over his, but she didn't let them linger. "I should sneak out before I get caught. That would be bad."

He rubbed his chin with his thumb and forefinger. "I'm struggling to understand why you're important to this picture. Why Preston brought Jim into all of this. I mean, how does he even know Jim? It's not like we introduced them. This is an elaborate plan to push me out. Too elaborate. There are easier ways. Nothing makes any sense."

"I don't have the answers to those questions. But I do have an idea."

"What's that?"

"Callie."

Reid tilted his head. "That's not an idea. That's your sister-in-law."

"Aren't you cute?" She patted his cheek. "Jagar said it's perfectly legal for Sally to do what she's doing because you own the company. The contract you have with your employees states anything on those servers becomes the company's property, and you and Preston have legal access."

"I love listening to you talk, but get to the point."

"Hire Callie."

"I'm one step ahead of you. She's already got her nose in all of this. It was Jagar's idea. I forgot to tell you."

She smacked his chest. "Don't forget shit like that. It pisses me off."

"I know." He chuckled.

"I don't find that funny." Wrapping her arms around his strong frame, she went in for one more kiss. All she wanted to do was get off this yacht and take him out on her sailboat and disappear for a week. If they got through this and he decided to stick around, she'd ask him to do it.

What did she have to lose?

"Go get some sleep," he whispered. "And be careful."

"You, too. And act normal. Even around Jim."

"That's going to be impossible when I want to string him up by his balls."

"When this is over, you'll have to wait in line." She snuck out of the guest room, and as quickly as possible, made her way down to the crew cabins.

Just as she rounded the corner in the mess hall, she ran into Craig.

"Hey, what are you doing up?" he asked as he poured himself a cup of coffee.

"Couldn't sleep. Are you headed up to anchor watch?"

"Shift starts at four, and we know how cranky Bradley gets if you're not there like five minutes early." He waved his coffee and headed back up the stairs.

Darcie snagged a bottle of water from the fridge and scurried down the hall. She pushed open the door and pulled it closed, gently.

It clicked.

Milia sighed and rolled. "What time is it?"

"Late." Darcie plugged in her cell and got between the sheets on the bottom bunk.

Four hours of sleep. That's all she needed.

"I tried waiting up for you," Milia said.

"Sorry. I got pre-occupied." Oh God. The last thing she needed was girl-bonding time.

"That's okay. But I want to talk to you about something," Milia said. "How would Jim know Preston?"

She blinked her eyes open. "He wouldn't. Not that I know of, why?"

"I saw them in an intense discussion right before

186

I went to bed. I wouldn't have thought it strange, but everything about this charter feels wrong." Milia leaned over the side of the top bunk. "Kim said the captain is acting very weird, and not in a good way considering they just got engaged. I know you probably don't want to hear about that or talk about it, but you've known Jim a long time, and Kim is not only worried about him, she's also concerned that something is wrong."

Right. Kim is just realizing that her fiancé has a wandering eye. "If she's worried about me, tell her she's got nothing to be jealous of. But I still stand by what I said about Jim. He's a slime, and I should have known. He's done it to every woman I've ever known him to date."

"Then why did you go out with him?"

"I got horny. I was bored. He said all the right things when I was vulnerable. And the worst part about that is he knew it."

"Knew what?"

"My history with Reid. He was there when Reid and I broke up, and Jim used it to get me into bed."

"Did you know Jim was engaged once before?"

"Jim was engaged? To who? When?" Darcie asked.

"Last year. And it was to some girl that worked with Anastasia."

"I thought this was the first time Anastasia worked with Jim," Darcie said.

Malia yawned. "It is. Anastasia didn't put it all together until she got a random text from her friend, who said Jim called off the wedding three weeks after they got engaged because he just wasn't marriage material. Kim's afraid he's going to do the same thing to her."

"I hate to say it, but she's probably right."

Her phone buzzed.

Reid: Make it to your room ok?

"I need to get a few hours of sleep. I'll talk to you in the morning."

"Thanks, Darcie."

"For what?"

"For always being so understanding. You come off intimidating at first, but you're really a nice person."

"So are you." She reached up and patted Malia's hand before snuggling back down in her bunk.

Darcie: I did, thanks for asking.

Reid: I'm sorry I dragged you into all of this.

Darcie: You didn't.

Reid: I want you to know if something bad happens to me that I never stopped loving you.

Darcie: Nothing bad is going to happen. And I never stopped either.

Reid: I should have said that before you left.

Darcie: You were never very good at doing that.

Reid: I'm hoping to get better at it if you'll give me a second chance.

She inhaled sharply, clutching the phone to her chest. She wanted that more than anything.

Darcie: You live in Texas. I live on a sailboat.

Reid: Details to be worked out.

Darcie: Good night, Reid.

Reid: Sleep well.

Darcie closed her eyes. Her heart tightened. Her mind whirled with a million possibilities, and for the first time in her life, she didn't look at each path with fear and trepidation. She didn't want to run and hide from what overwhelmed her anymore, she wanted to embrace the challenge.

She smiled, feeling she might actually understand what it meant to be a thrill seeker.

CHAPTER 10

*a*bout the only way to appease Reid's rage was to find an outlet for it, and that required getting an adrenaline rush moving through his body.

Or getting drunk.

The latter wasn't a good idea at seven in the morning.

He stood on the aft deck where they kept all the toys.

Kids' toys.

The problem with extreme sports was that it wasn't worth it unless he was traveling at ridiculously high speeds.

Those fucking jet skis weren't worth it.

However, sticking his fist through Jim's face might do the trick.

Who the fuck tracked down a woman, wooed her into his bed, and then cheated on her, all because Preston Jenner asked him to? No. Preston had to have something on Jim. Something big and juicy.

Or Jim was just a dick.

Which was a possibility.

"You are up bright and early," Craig said. "Though I'm not surprised the rest of your group is still sleeping. They sure know how to tie one on."

"They will be up by nine. Preston will make sure of it. But I can't sleep that late, and I thought this morning was too beautiful to waste."

"I totally agree. And the water won't stay like glass for long. This is the perfect time to go skiing. Darcie's bringing the tender around. We've got three wakeboards for you to choose from."

"I picked that one." He pointed to one he'd pulled from the pile. "I'll go without a wetsuit. And yes, I know I have to wear a life vest."

The sound of a motor cutting through the water caught his attention. Darcie sat in the middle of the center console wearing a tight, V-neck sun shirt and tiny black shorts that barely covered her adorable little ass.

That moved some blood around in his system.

He watched with a smile tugging at his lips as she maneuvered the small motorboat with ease. He climbed on the back, wishing he could pull her in for an embrace. Or maybe find a small nook offshore for a little morning hanky-panky.

But Craig, the spotter, put a damper on that. Yachting and all their rules.

"You're going to regret not wearing a wetsuit." She tossed him the handle as she idled away from the yacht.

"I like my water refreshing," Reid said as he pulled the straps on his lifejacket tight.

"I'm not a guy, but correct me if I'm wrong, Craig, it's the kind of cold that causes massive shrinkage, right?"

"She's not lying." Craig took a seat next to Darcie, facing backward. "It's totally embarrassing, dude."

Reid stuck his hand over the side, feeling the water. It was a bit on the chilly side, but he wasn't backing out now.

"You can hop in whenever you're ready." She pointed toward the shore. "We'll go up and down in that little cove right there."

It had been a good two years since he'd been wakeboarding, but it had to be like bike riding.

He hoped. It would suck to wipe out in front of Darcie during a leisurely morning ski run.

He climbed on the back platform, greased the boots, and slipped his feet in. "Here goes nothing."

His body hit the water, and within a second, it felt like an elephant sat on his chest. He popped his head out and gasped for air. "Holy motherfucker. You can put it in gear."

"Is it cold?" She tossed her arm over the back of the bench and rested her chin in her hand.

"Can you please hit it?" he said with his teeth chattering.

"Put the man out of his misery," Craig said.

She pushed the throttle down, and as soon as the rope pulled taut, she took the boat up to speed.

He popped out of the water quickly, but it took a little while for the sun to warm him up, and he took it easy on the tricks because he didn't want to fall back into what felt like a damned ice cube tray. He stuck with basic flips and things he knew he could do in his sleep. Wasn't very thrilling, but he got that when his balls hit his throat and when he nearly froze to death.

It also woke him up and gave him a chance to clear his head from everything he'd learned, which wasn't nearly enough. It posed more questions than it gave answers.

The sound of a couple of jet skis approaching caught his attention.

He hit a wave funky and wiped out when he realized it was Preston and one of the team members. At least this time the water didn't feel so frigid. He swam to the wakeboard and rested his arms over the top. "He is not going to splash me," Reid muttered.

"I believe that is his intention." Darcie stood, turning the steering wheel and tapping the throttle, maneuvering the boat between him and the approaching jet ski.

Craig waved his hands up in the air.

"Y'all are very rule-oriented." Reid handed Craig the wakeboard and climbed up onto the boat. "Not that I wanted to get sprayed." The reality of what was going down crawled back into his brain, and he didn't even know the half of it yet. "Or get knocked in the head."

"That was some of the lamest, most boring tricks I've ever seen," Preston said. He pulled up alongside the motorboat and cut the engine. "You looked like an old man out there."

"I'm not getting any younger," Reid said.

"Well, this youngster wants to give it a whirl, and I'd like to have a few words with you over an Irish coffee."

Reid knew he couldn't avoid Preston or the team all day, and even though he still had files to go through and try to make sense of, he wouldn't be able to hole up in his room and do that all day either. "What if I wasn't done yet?"

"You're done," Preston said. "Give him the keys to the jet ski."

There was nothing worse than being spoken to like a child by your business partner in front of a team member, but Reid had no choice. He had to let it go.

For now.

He took the key and climbed on the watercraft. "Thanks for the morning ride."

"Our pleasure," Darcie said. "See you back at the yacht."

Reid gunned the jet ski and took off, moving full speed ahead, which was only about sixty-five miles an hour. He went in a straight line, not doing even a single doughnut. It took him all of maybe eight minutes to get back to the vessel where Bradley helped him off the watercraft and took his life vest.

"Did you have fun out there?"

"I did, thank you," Reid said.

"And you, sir?" Bradley asked.

"Not as fun as this one." He smacked Reid on the back. "I think he has the hots for your boson."

"I've got no comment on that." Bradley tossed the life jackets to the corner. "There are some muffins out if you want to start on those before breakfast is served."

"Thanks. We just might do that." Preston put his arm around Reid. "Let's go upstairs."

Reid shrugged Preston's hand away as soon as they were standing in the main aft deck where the interior had set up a nice continental buffet.

The sun shone brightly over the mountains, and the wind rippled across the water below. If Reid weren't preparing for battle, this might have been a nice day.

"Let's stop pretending we like each other when no one is around," Reid said.

"You're still mad at me for last night." Preston poured two large mugs of coffee and snagged a chocolate muffin. He pointed to the lounge chairs by the hot tub where he must have been earlier since his computer and a few folders were on the table.

Reid's mood had gone from mildly okay—but only because Darcie had been in close proximity—to completely foul in a matter of seconds, and he didn't see it getting any better. "Of course, I am."

"I was wasted. I'm sorry."

"You lied to me. And that wasn't when you were drunk."

"I didn't want to burst your bubble," Preston said. "You were so excited about the fire department and a potential deal with them, I didn't want to ruin it. I finally had my old partner back. I hadn't seen that side of you in years. I didn't want to let him go. But then Darcie showed up and it's like you can't think straight again."

"Darcie isn't the problem."

Preston crossed his legs at the ankles as he broke off a small piece of muffin and placed it into his mouth. He chewed and swallowed as if he were eating a million-dollar meal.

Or maybe his last meal.

That would be nice.

"Maybe not. I have no idea. All I know is that I have been working my ass off for the last year trying to save our company, while you have been doing nothing but pining over a woman who isn't worth it. And what's worse, before that, you checked out while dating Darcie. And even *before* that." Preston waved his hand dramatically in the air. "You had to go and have feelings for my sister. Well, Darcie isn't half the girl my sister was."

"Is that what this is about? You don't like Darcie because you think she replaced Erin or something?"

"No. This is about you fucking up and me having to make decisions, and now you want to come back in and change things, and I'm not having it. We are moving in a new direction. My direction."

"What does that mean, exactly?"

"It means we're moving out of the safety-only

business and moving into the money-making business."

"Oh, please. We make a lot of fucking money at what we do. Or do I need to remind you of your salary?"

"Nope. But think about what we could do with Hans if we mass-marketed more of our extreme safety equipment like our line for snorkeling."

"That was the dumbest thing we've ever done," Reid said.

"Because we didn't do it right. Reid can help tailor each of our products that are for the extremists or for stunt doubles and make them for everyday people. That's where the real money is."

"But we were never about the money. We were always about safety, and this flame-resistant suit for the firefighters could be a game-changer. It's what we built this company on."

"No. I was never on board with that direction, and it could also bankrupt us. It will never be a product line that even breaks even. I've been crunching the numbers. It's not worth pursuing outside of the stunt business or the extreme sports world."

"We have enough money to give back. We could do the deal with the fire departments if the suits are viable."

"No. We can't. The testing alone will kill us. Again. I'm the one who has been doing all the data accumulation and research while you've been dealing with a broken heart over a girl who didn't give a shit about you." Preston sipped his coffee and glanced around. "I heard she had an affair with the captain of this vessel not a month ago, and he's engaged to someone else."

"And where did you hear that?" Reid couldn't believe he was having this conversation. It was as if they were two teenage girls in middle school.

Worse, he now had to accept the absolute worst about his business partner.

And friend.

Who had never truly been his friend to begin with.

"The crew on this boat likes to gossip."

Now that was really fucking funny because the deckhands didn't. Or at least they didn't seem to since they appeared to have a lot of respect for Darcie. Reid couldn't imagine any of them talking shit about her behind her back.

The interior, while he could see that they could be catty, he still didn't buy it.

Of course, there was Jim. Fucking asshole.

And the fact that this entire trip was a damn setup.

"Have you already signed contracts with Hans?" Reid asked. Thus far, he hadn't found any on the mirrored server, which in his mind was good, but that didn't mean they weren't moving forward. And without patents and proof the technology would work, none of it mattered.

"We did a licensing deal. Yes. We are making fire-resistant bedsheets, comforters, and window treatments."

"There is no approval for this. No proof that our product works. We don't even know if we can scale it down."

"The patent is pending, and that's all the proof we need. Besides, we're not claiming it won't catch fire, we're just saying it will take a little while longer—which we know with the suits is true. And it's not like we're not the first company out there to claim this."

"Oh, and that makes it okay?"

"I really don't understand why you're getting so upset."

"You should have told me this the other day when I asked. Hell, I should have been involved from the very beginning. Especially when we said we wouldn't bring this to a mass-market level."

"We never said that." Preston waved a folder between the two of them. "For years, we've done things mostly your way. I've always had to either design the product first and get you excited, or just let you be pissed at me until the money came rolling in."

"We had this discussion last night. It got us nowhere."

"I was drunk. I didn't articulate myself well, and I didn't have these." He handed him the folder.

"What's this?"

"The financial health of our company. Its growth. Projections. Both past and present. It shows that in the last year, basically while you've been drinking yourself to death over Darcie, I've increased our profits nearly twenty percent. I've also taken a few random employee polls that are very telling, as well."

"And what exactly does that express?" Reid didn't need to be told the answer. He knew. He felt it every time he walked into the office. He'd thought that, over time, things would turn around, and his people would learn to trust him again.

Especially since he and Preston were working well together.

But that had all been a farce, and Preston had planned on kicking him to the curb all along.

"That our people are more productive and happier when I'm at the helm," Preston said.

"You can make numbers present themselves one

way or the other," Reid said. He knew how to play the game. However, he was sure there was some truth to the statement. Reid had checked out of so many things for the last year that he honestly hadn't a clue what deals Preston had been negotiating or even what new products were being developed. He'd been playing catch-up and not very well.

"I made no analysis. Just black and white. And you have to admit, you and I are constantly butting heads."

"I'll admit it's been a rough year, but I thought we'd cleared up our differences two months ago." Reid wanted the business to succeed because he wanted to honor Erin. But Preston only wanted to use the memory of his sister to make money. And long before Darcie came into the picture, Reid had been pulling back from his responsibilities. It had become a constant battle to keep Preston from going off the deep end.

So, why the hell was Reid even sitting here listening to this bullshit?

Darcie.

His company.

His life's work.

It's why he'd come back in the first place. He'd lost everything, and it was high time he got his shit together and gained his life back.

Only, he might have opened his eyes too late to save his company.

Hopefully, it wasn't too late for him and Darcie.

"I placated you when you decided you wanted to work again," Preston said.

"Why would you do that if you planned on running me out?" Reid pushed his glasses up over his head. "And don't try to deny it. I know that's what you're doing."

"You could save me the time and energy and just sell me your half."

"I could, but I don't give up that easily."

"No. You don't. And neither do I." Preston snagged a different set of papers. "We started our company because we wanted to make products so we could almost die but not quite. We create the illusion of safety in an industry filled with idiots who have death wishes."

"Are you describing yourself?"

"You know I am, only I want to live to tell about it. I get off on pushing my body to the extreme. The extremist is a rare individual. But there is an entire group of people who—"

"Here we go again." Reid flipped through the pages of the proposal with Hans. "How many times are you going to lecture me on theme parks, rollercoaster rides, and how to capitalize on that market? Because we'd be spreading ourselves too thin."

"This isn't a lecture. I'm telling you what's going on with Hans. Why we're really having this meeting."

A couple of the team members strolled by in swim trunks. They waved but knew better than to stop and chat. They climbed into the hot tub, with their backs turned.

Milia appeared through the main salon doors holding a pot of fresh coffee. "Can I get you boys anything?"

"You can certainly freshen me up." Preston held out his mug.

"Me, too."

Milia nodded. "Will you be ready for breakfast in about a half-hour?"

"Sounds wonderful," Preston said.

"Captain Jim says we will be pulling up anchor after lunch to head to our next spot. Until then, it looks like the deck crew has all the toys out so if there is anything you need, just let us know."

"Thanks. You all are great." Preston set his mug on the table.

Reid continued scanning the paperwork. His heart pounded so fast he couldn't tell where one beat ended and the next one started. He'd really been in la-la land if this is what his business partner had been up to. "Jesus," he whispered. "When Darcie and I broke up, you told me to take all the time I needed to get my shit together. You acted like you actually cared about me. But you didn't. You just wanted time to do this." Fuck. How stupid could he have been?

"I saw an opportunity." Preston reached out and tapped the documents. "That's a solid plan."

"It's not what our company is about. And last night you went off half-cocked, using Erin's death as a motivator to get me on board with taking the fire-resistant material to manufacturing, when that's only one very tiny part of this deal."

"It's the part that makes us look really good in the eyes of the consumer. The cost is minimal to make the resistant fabric."

"You don't know this. We haven't tested... Jesus. You had Hans do it already, didn't you?"

"He's been working with a different company for years. They upped the prices last year, and the quality isn't as good. Hans has eight new casinos opening in the next two years. He wants some kind of extreme sports booth at each one. We can also run extreme sports expeditions out of some of the locations using all of our equipment, brands, employees...you name it. This isn't just about getting into the flame-resistant business. And it's not contingent on the fire suits with the fire department, though that's what opened the door. This is about building an empire. Don't you see the beauty in it?"

Reid stood. Taking his coffee, he waltzed to the shore side of the boat. Below, Darcie tossed a line from the tender to one of the other deckhands. Two more of the team hopped onto the back of the motorboat to go skiing. Reid had to wonder what, if anything, those boys knew about the issues between him and Preston. If they knew Reid wanted nothing to do with the likes of Hans or his greed.

"Actually, I don't," Reid said. "And I don't understand what is driving you. Is it really money? Because you've got more than enough. And fame? You are well-known in this industry, so I don't get why you're doing this."

"I don't get why you wouldn't," Preston said, joining him at the railing. "We're thrill seekers. We have been our entire lives. It's what we were born to do, and we can bring it to anyone who wants to give it a go. Isn't that what our company does? Isn't that what we started?"

"Yes." Reid couldn't deny that's what they did and would continue doing. "But this plan you have going with Hans, it's not our vision. This is all about taking people's money. It's not about giving them an experience."

"It absolutely is. And I plan on doing it as safely as possible, which is our bottom line."

"You're really blurring the lines."

"No. I'm not," Preston said. "It's all pretty simple. It comes down to the fact that I'm doing it with or without you. It's your choice."

"You've broken our articles of incorporation as well as our partnership agreement, and I'm guessing since you're about to go to bed with Hans, you've broken a law or two also."

"So sue me. Or leave. Again, your choice. I'm just tired of this game we've been playing. I thought it would be easy to fall back into it. Hell, I was even having a little fun with you, but I'm seriously over it. We're not friends. We haven't been since you got tangled up with my sister. I don't want to work with you anymore, but it's not that simple to cut you out of the business."

"No. Certain things would have to happen," Reid said. "And I'm not leaving."

"Looks like we're going into business together with Hans, then."

"No. We're not," Reid said. "You need my signature."

"Remember when I told you to take all the time in the world after Darcie dumped you and you gave me permission to do what I needed without you having to sign every little thing?"

Reid eyed one of the jet skis as it hit a massive wave and rose up at least three feet into the air. His teammate misjudged the way the WaveRunner would land, and the watercraft spun to the right, dumping the young man. Reid felt like he'd just crashed and burned. "I might have left you to run things for a while, but you couldn't pull off a deal like that with Hans, or anyone else, completely behind my back. Which breaks our partnership agreement. Which would dissolve our company. I don't think you or Hans want that, considering what it would do to your deal."

"Nope. That would kind of shut things down." Preston folded his arms. "I brought you on this trip to fuck you over."

"You don't say."

"We can do this the easy way or the hard way. Give me this deal and we find a way to co-exist. Or you walk. You have until our meeting with Hans tonight to decide." Preston slapped Reid on the back. "Keep the paperwork, and I emailed you everything ever discussed on the deal to get you up to speed."

Reid inhaled sharply, catching the mix of fresh sea air and bitter coffee. It soured his stomach. Neither choice was a good option.

"And If I refuse to do either?" Reid asked.

"Then you've left me with no choice." Preston strolled across the deck and snagged the last folder. "I didn't want to have to resort to this, but I will."

"What are you talking about? Resort to what?" Reid rolled his neck, cracking it twice.

"Your little girlfriend has broken maritime law, not to mention she's been in breach of her contract more than once during this charter. This is the proof that Captain Jim has compiled."

"You're bluffing." Reid lunged forward.

Preston yanked his hand back. "I most certainly am not. You don't give me what I want, her yachting career is over. Not to mention, Jim has to call the Coast Guard because of the illegal drugs she has on board."

"That's bullshit. She would never. You'd be framing her." Reid's heart hammered in his chest. He didn't believe that Preston was bluffing. Not one bit. He knew without a doubt that if push came to shove, Preston would cut Darcie up into tiny little pieces and toss her overboard as shark bait.

"And you," Preston said with a wicked smile, "did you enjoy yourself last night? I bet Darcie is a good little fuck."

"You mother—"

Milia stepped out onto the aft deck. "Excuse me,

but can I take an egg order? Or do you want some pancakes? French toast?"

"Oh, how about you have that chef whip up a little bit of everything," Preston said. "Sound good, Reid?"

"I've got some reading to do." Reid snatched the files.

"So, you're going to get on board with Hans?"

"Looks like you've left me with no choice."

Over his fucking dead body would he let Preston get away with any of this.

CHAPTER 11

*D*arcie smiled. "Hey, you." She glanced around, taking Reid by the hand and tugging him into the corner. She leaned in to steal a quick kiss, but he pushed her away.

"Are you crazy?" His gaze darted everywhere but at her.

"No one is around."

"Not the point. We can't do that." He ran a hand through his thick hair.

"I'm going on break in a little bit. I can sneak into your cabin." She winked.

"I don't think we should be doing that."

"Preston certainly put you in a foul mood. Why don't you let me fix that?" She leaned closer, letting her hand rest on the inside of his thigh.

He batted it away. "Stop. I mean it. We can't be fooling around. We made a mistake."

She opened her mouth, but no words formed. She snapped her jaw and tried again.

Nothing.

She cleared her throat.

Still. Nothing.

This couldn't be happening. Not again. It was like someone flipped a switch, and Reid went from kind and loving to some angry stranger. This is what he'd done right before they broke up a year ago, and it had Preston written all over it.

She wasn't going to let that asshole ruin things again.

"We made a mistake? Or Preston got into your head?" She planted her hands on her hips and glared. "What the fuck did he say to you?

"He has nothing to do with this. We just got caught up in a whirlwind of seeing each other again, and now I have a shit ton of stuff to deal with regarding this meeting tonight and I need to read all this stuff." He waved a bunch of papers. "I can't mess this deal up. It's important to my company."

"Oh. My. God. Are you fucking kidding me?" She curled her fingers around his wrist and dragged him to his room where she kicked open the door and slammed it behind them. "Do you mind telling me where this is coming from? Because a few hours ago we were—"

"I know what we were doing, and I've had a change of heart."

"Oh. No. You are not doing that. And not just to me. Hell, I don't give a shit about that. Well, I do, but you are not letting Preston push you around. Whatever he told you just now, he's just doing it to manipulate you."

"Get out of my room, Darcie. You're in over your head, and whatever we thought we could fix, we can't. Let it go."

She narrowed her eyes. "Like hell I will. And I'm not going to stand here and let you just give up or let him fuck with you anymore."

He held up a bottle of whiskey, screwed off the cap, and took a shot. "I'm going to take a quick shower, grab my computer, and then join my team. We've got some work to discuss and then some major partying to do."

"Don't do this, Reid. You're going to regret it."

"You're probably right, but it's my life to fuck up, now isn't it?"

She poked him in the chest. "I'm not letting you do this to yourself. Whatever he's got on you, we'll deal with it. Together. I'm not giving up." She turned on her heels and stormed off with her stomach growling. She needed a few moments to calm down. She'd get something to eat and then she'd talk some sense into that man.

She found the fixings for her favorite sandwich and got to work while Kirk lounged at the table with a book.

"How are you holding up this morning?" Kirk asked.

"Exhausted."

"I need to tell you something." Kirk sat up and glanced around. "The entire boat knows you were in Reid's room last night."

"Excuse me?" Darcie took her grilled cheese and slid behind the table, hiding her shaking hands. "I have no idea what you're talking about."

"Anastasia overheard Reid's team members telling Preston they saw you coming out of his cabin and wondered if you were a cokehead like Reid."

"What?" Her voice rose a couple of octaves. "First off, I don't do drugs, and while Reid likes to drink and always has, he's never even smoked pot. I know this because I have, and I tried to get him to take a hit, and he wouldn't."

"I asked Anastasia if she could have misunderstood, but she said Bradley heard some shit too."

"From Preston and Reid's team?"

Kirk nodded.

"Have you heard anything specific?"

"No. But I'll be honest, I'm going to be listening now."

"Good. I want you to, and I want you to tell me everything. But don't say a thing to Captain Jim." She picked up her radio. "Bradley. Bradley. This is Darcie. Can you meet me in the crew mess?"

"On my way," Bradley said over the radio.

"Do me a favor and go find Anastasia and ask her not to tell Malia. I just don't know if I can trust her or not with the whole Kim and Jim thing, and I don't trust Jim right now as far as I can spit."

"The captain's acting weird. He's staying in the bridge more than usual, and he seems nervous," Kirk said. "This entire charter has a weird vibe. And for the record, I would never think you did drugs, but it's kind of obvious that you and that Reid guy have the hots for each other."

"He's my ex-boyfriend. I did at one time think he was the sexiest man alive," she said, not hiding her smile. "Actually, I still do."

"I wouldn't kick him out of bed."

"Kick who out of bed?" Bradley asked as he snagged an apple.

"Reid," Kirk said.

"I don't think anyone in their right mind, straight or gay, would ask him to leave. Now Preston, doesn't matter how good-looking he is or ripped his abs are, that man is a douchebag."

"I totally agree," Darcie said. "I need to ask you about what Reid and Preston's team is saying about me. And Reid."

"Am I allowed to speak freely and as frankly as possible? As if you're not my boson?" Bradley asked.

She nodded.

"Are you sure? Because there is only one way to put this, and it's not pretty."

"I'm sure."

"They're just idiots who are jealous that their boss is getting a little action and they're only riding jet skis with governors on them."

She had to appreciate the man's honesty. "Do you think they are saying these things purposefully in earshot of you all?"

"Who knows with people like that," Kirk said. "Half the time, they act as if we're not even around, unless they need something."

"True," she said. "Alrighty. Just let me know what else you hear, okay."

"You got it." Bradley turned and jogged back up the stairs.

"I better get back out there before my boson tells me I'm slacking." Kirk knocked on the table with his knuckles. "See you later."

She picked at her sandwich and stared at her computer screen. Reid didn't do cocaine any more than she did. So,why would his team say that he did? And why would they be gossiping about her sneaking out of his room?

Of course, that was cause for dismissal. But what would having her fired in the middle of a charter do for Preston? And she wouldn't actually be let go until they docked. She let out a long breath. She had a million questions with no answers.

She opened her laptop and pulled up the portal to the miscellaneous files from Reid's server. It bothered her to no end that Jim had been communicating with Preston for months. It didn't fit in her mind that whatever this was, it had been planned out months ago when Jim first contacted her to be his boson.

And then his bunkmate.

Why?

She pinched the bridge of her nose. "Fuck it." She slammed the laptop closed and ran up the steps, turned the corner, and ran up the second flight, right into the bridge.

"What the fuck?" Captain Jim said as he swiveled in his big brown leather chair. "You scared the shit out of me."

"Sorry, but we need to talk."

"It's going to have to wait. We'll be anchoring soon, and I've got work to do."

"Why'd you call me to be your boson?"

"Because I needed a good one, and I heard you were between jobs. You know how small the industry is."

"Nice standard, well-rehearsed answer. But I'm not buying it." She set her computer down on the table by the stairs. "Tell me what the fuck is going on."

"With?" Jim stared at her with wide eyes.

"Me. You. This fucking charter. Everything. It doesn't add up."

"You're not making sense." He placed both hands on her shoulders and lowered his chin. "Are you feeling okay? Is something wrong? You've been acting off for the last two days."

She opened her mouth and then snapped it shut.

"Maybe you should go lie down. I can have Kirk take over your responsibilities for the rest of this charter if things are too much for you," Jim said.

"Are you kidding me?"

"When I found out Reid was coming on board, I thought about asking you to sit on the sidelines. I know you're a tough girl, but with all that transpired over the last twenty-four hours, I think it's best—"

"Oh, shut the fuck up." That went nowhere fast,

and she quickly realized the error of her ways. Whatever was going on with Jim, he was too far gone to reason with at this juncture. She snagged her laptop.

He grabbed her arms.

"You're out of control, and your eyes are bloodshot. Did you even sleep last night?"

Motherfucker. "No. I didn't," she admitted. "Anything else? Do you want to drug test me? I'll pee in a cup right now, no problem."

"That won't be necessary."

"I didn't think so." She tucked her computer under her arm and jogged down the stairs then marched herself into her cabin and slammed the door. Only there was no space to pace in her room. "Fuck. Fuck. Fuck."

"What?" Milia popped her head out from under her blanket. "What's wrong?"

"Sorry. I didn't know you were in here."

"I'm on a break, and I'm hiding with my nose in a book."

"Hiding from what?"

"Can I be honest?"

Darcie let out a long sigh. "Please. I'd appreciate it."

"I don't like these people. They say weird things in hushed tones, but it's obvious they want me to know what they are saying, and it's all bad things about you and Reid. Things that I know, at least with you, aren't true. And with the way Jim is acting and Kim constantly texting me, wanting to know what is going on, well, I just want this season to be over."

"You and me both." Darcie climbed into her bunk. She hooked up her phone to her charger and checked the time. She still had another half-hour on her break. She'd use the time to look at more of the files and emails from the server. She glanced at her text thread with Reid.

Nothing.

Well, he had a lot on his mind. She had to believe that he hadn't meant the harsh words he'd said earlier. Whatever had transpired between him and Preston had fucked with his head something good. She just needed to give him some time to sort it all out. And it didn't help that they were stuck out at sea.

She squared her shoulders and pulled up the folder labeled: *Operation Dream.*

It seemed like a weird descriptor for both Reid and Preston. Neither of them were dreamers. They considered themselves doers. Go-getters. Not dreamers. That term was reserved for people who thought about shit but never went about doing it.

An argument she used to love having with Reid when they'd been dating.

There were three documents in the folder. There were named:

Plan A.

Plan B.

Reid's Note.

She clicked on Reid's Note.

"I'm sorry Kim is struggling," Darcie said, feeling a little bad that she'd basically ignored that part of the conversation.

"I think I made a mistake by supporting her decision to be with Jim."

"Nah. That's what friends are for, and she needs a good one by her side no matter what happens."

"You don't think Jim is capable of changing his spots, do you?"

"I don't know." If she were being totally honest with herself, she thought that Jim could be a kind and loving man. And with the right woman, maybe he would be a wonderful partner.

Plus, Kim was kind of perfect for him. She had all the qualities he liked in a woman, especially the part where she followed him around like a pathetic puppy, hanging on his every word.

That was the disconnect with her relationship with Jim. She was just too damn independent for a man with his tastes. He liked to be the big man calling all the shots for his little lady.

That didn't work for Darcie, but it worked for Kim.

"Is Kim happy?" Darcie asked.

"No. Not really. She pretends to be. She wants to be. I mean, he swept her off her feet. But since she left the boat, he's been distant and acting weird."

"Maybe it's not her. Maybe he has other issues." What the bloody hell? Now she was defending him? As if he were caught in the crossfire with all this? Fuck, no. "Or maybe he's just an asshole, and she should dump him."

"That's what I want to tell her."

"I wish my friends had told me that," Darcie said. "My family members were the only ones willing to get in my face when it came to Jim."

"What about Reid? What did they think of Reid?"

"They all loved him. Still do. If I took him back, they'd throw a fucking party."

"Why don't the two of you get back together, then?"

"Because people like Jim and Preston always get in the way," Darcie admitted as she clicked on *Reid's Note*. "I wish I had some good advice to give you to forward on to Kim, but I don't know what to think of Jim these days. And my opinion is severely skewed in the negative."

"Well, I think Kim is going to be asking for a long engagement if she doesn't call the whole thing off."

"Whatever she does, she shouldn't make any rash decisions. And if she wants, tell her she can call me once this charter is over." Oh for fuck's sake, why would Darcie offer herself up like that?

Because she was a kind and decent woman, who needed to believe that in a week, this entire thing would be over, and all the questions she had would be answered, and she'd be sleeping full-time in Reid's bed.

She had to believe that.

Had to.

Otherwise, she'd go crazy.

"Thanks." Malia rolled over and went back to her book.

Darcie focused on the file she opened. *Reid's Note.* Her pulse increased as she read the words on the screen.

To Whom It May Concern:

I've never understood that greeting. What does it mean? Does it mean people might not be concerned? Well, in my case, that is absolutely true. I'm not worth being concerned about.

What the fuck? Of course, he was worth it, and

he knew it. Why would he even write a note suggesting that he wasn't? And why the fuck would he put it on this server?

Reid wouldn't.

She sat up straight, hitting her head on the top bunk. "Fuck."

"Are you okay?" Milia asked.

"Just ducky," she said, flicking her finger over the trackpad. This didn't make sense.

My life has been one bad turn after the next, and I've grown tired of it. It's time to put an end to it. I can't live like this any longer.

Darcie blinked. She knew that Reid could be weird and moody and emotional, but this didn't sound like him at all.

I've turned my company into the one thing Erin would be most disappointed in. I don't know how it happened. Or when it turned. Yes, I do. It was the first time I tried cocaine. That's when everything changed.

What the hell?

Darcie introduced me to the devil. We danced together, and for a while. it was good. Until it wasn't.

Like most things with Darcie.

Jesus.

Erin once told me that you come into this world in a blaze of glory. A mad adrenaline rush, and some of us are wired to cling to that emotion for the rest of our lives, unable to be satisfied with that one wild journey into the simplicity of living because our hearts are never settled. These tortured souls are restless and can never tame the beast. Enough is never enough. In the land of the living, life should be the end game.

But in my world, it's that split second between life and death where you know you're a goner and yet you straddle the space between. That's the moment no one can live to tell about, and that's the moment all true extremists live for.

I've accepted the fact that I'm like Erin, a true extremist, and I can't deny the need to experience the one second between life and death.

See you on the flip side.

"No. No. No fucking way." Darcie jumped from her bed. "This can't be happening."

"What? What's wrong?" Milia asked.

"Everything."

WITH A SHAKY HAND, Reid opened the last file that Preston had given him and stared at what he knew to be doctored images of Darcie with a line of cocaine. He flipped to another picture of him and Darcie, taken a year or so ago, showing them drinking with what appeared to be a white powdery substance on the table.

Photoshopped in, of course.

But the worst was seeing all the drugs stashed in her cabin and on her sailboat.

There were even pictures of her and Jim with suitcases full of drugs as they transported them onto the superyacht, which explained how Captain Jim had become involved.

The only question was: had Jim done so willingly, or was Preston using him, as well?

"Fuck." Reid tossed the folders across the room. They hit the porthole and scattered to the floor. He was fucking screwed.

And if he didn't do what Preston wanted, Darcie would lose everything.

He couldn't allow that to happen. She had her entire life ahead of her, and he had one foot on the downslope. He slumped to the side of the bed and cradled his face in his hands. He'd made a mess of his life all because he'd had a fear of abandonment.

His parents, while loving, had never really understood him, nor had they been there for him.

He used thrill seeking as a way to hold onto his humanity. To feel something. Anything. He also used it to keep people at arm's length. He never wanted to get too close, and when he did, it never ended well.

However, in this case, he had no one to blame but himself.

And he had no idea what to do.

But he couldn't sit idly by and do nothing, and he couldn't tell Darcie. Not this time.

He picked up his cell and called Jagar.

"What's up, man?"

"I'm only calling out of respect for you." Reid put the phone on speaker and placed it on the side of the bed.

"I don't like the sound of that," Jagar said.

"Preston has me between a rock and a hard place, and in order to protect those I care about, I need to sell my soul to the devil."

"You fucking bastard. I'm not letting you break my little sister's heart again."

Reid rubbed his temple. "She'll be fine, especially after how I behaved this afternoon."

"What does that mean?"

"I've already started by telling her I thought us being together was a mistake, and I'm going to get drunk and belligerent and act like a fool."

"And why are we going to do this?"

"Because if I don't, Preston is going to make your sister out to be a drug addict. Or worse. Say that she's selling drugs on the high seas and using the charter business to do it."

"How is he going to do that, exactly?" Jagar asked.

Reid stood, ran a hand through his hair, and took in a deep breath, trying to calm his out-of-control pulse. "He's got fake evidence. He's also creating a narrative. Fuck. My head hurts."

"Listen. I need you to relax a little."

"Right. I'm on a fucking boat that I can't get off with a goddamned crazy person who wants to not only ruin me, but also the woman I love. And he's been fucking with us from the beginning. I'm sorry if I'm a little pissed off at the moment."

"That's better than when you first called informing me that you were going to call it quits."

"Well, I don't know what else to do. I can't let him destroy Darcie's career."

"No. You can't. Let me get my detective brain working," Jagar said. "Can you send me the pictures."

"Sure. I can send you all the blackmail material he just gave me."

"Good."

Reid set all the papers out on the small desk and, using the document scanning app on his phone, he made copies and emailed them all to Jagar.

"This feels like such an elaborate plan where so many things could go wrong," Jagar said. "If Preston only wanted you to sign off on this deal—"

"This is about Preston getting off. You have to

remember that it's always first about the thrill with him. Everything else is secondary. He needs to live on the edge. To always be so close to danger that his heart rate is always elevated. It's like going through life with a semi-hard dick."

"I have to say that would suck."

"I know," Reid said. "Too much of a good thing is often a bad thing."

"Okay, but he still has something he wants to achieve, and I go back to him wanting this deal with Hans and wanting you out of the company doesn't equate to these elaborate plans that have been in the works for months. And that brings me to my sister. Callie's read the emails. I looked at the information you sent me. We're missing something."

Reid's door rattled. A second later, Darcie came barreling in, all out of breath.

She held up the computer, pointing at the screen. "He plans on...plans on...plans on..."

"Slow down and breathe." Reid took the laptop from her shaking hands and closed the door. "I've got your brother on speaker. Now what are you babbling on about?"

Her chest heaved. Her eyes were as big as golf balls as she waggled her finger. "Note. Fake. From Reid."

"Look at me." Reid took her by the biceps and

made eye contact. "In through the nose, and out through the mouth." He nodded as she inhaled sharply, then exhaled loudly. "That's it." He'd never known her to panic, so whatever had her spooked had to be something big. "Take your time."

"Jagar. You're going to need to get involved now."

"I already am," Jagar said.

"No. I mean officially."

Reid ran his thumb over her cheek, wiping away a single tear.

"Why? What happened?"

"I found a note on the server," Darcie said. "Preston plans on killing Reid and making it look like suicide."

"He's planning what?" Reid grabbed the computer.

"The best part is in your suicide note, you blame me for getting you hooked on cocaine."

The laptop slipped through his fingers and landed on his toes. "Fuck." He jumped up and down.

"I need a copy of that note and anything else you found," Jagar's voice crackled over the cell.

Reid picked up the computer and sat down at the desk. He waved to Darcie. "Get my cell," he said. "Jagar. You've already got copies. At least, Callie does. I'm texting you the file names and directories now." Reid clicked one of the other tabs and glanced over Preston's elaborate scheme to get back at Reid.

"Holy shit," Reid mumbled.

"What is it?" Darcie stood behind him with her hands on his shoulders.

"I thought he destroyed it."

"What?" Darcie repeated.

Reid reached out with a shaky hand and circled his finger over the screen. He couldn't bring himself to touch the words on the page.

"Erin's digital journal, and her suicide note." He split the screen between the note Preston had written pretending to be Reid and the one Erin had left behind. His stomach soured as he compared the two passages. Not completely identical, but close enough.

"And he used Erin's words to write mine."

CHAPTER 12

"Relax. Everything is going to be fine." Reid took Darcie into his arms and kissed her forehead. "Your brother and his friends are taking care of it."

"It's almost dinnertime. What if my brother can't get this all sorted out before this Hans guy shows up, and Preston wants to cart you off to your death?"

"That's not going to happen." At least Reid hoped that wasn't on the menu for dessert. Of course, he didn't know if he was scheduled to die by bungee failure or diving disaster. Either way, he had no intention of having his heart stop beating anytime soon.

"It better not. You owe me a proper feelings discussion," Darcie said.

He chuckled. "I owe you a lot of chats. One of

which includes my undying support of your career choice."

She arched a brow. "As a drug runner on the open seas?"

"Not even remotely funny." He tapped her nose.

"It still seems so batshit crazy to me that Preston would put so much time and energy into this wild, elaborate scheme. He could have fucked you over a variety of ways."

"But he wouldn't have had the satisfaction of hurting me through you, and we don't know what kind of fucked-up game he's playing with Jim. Are they are friends, or does Preston have something on Jim and is blackmailing him, as well?"

"Jim has always been motivated by money." She touched her ear. "I need to get out there."

"I don't like this last-minute change in dinner plans."

"I don't either," Darcie said. "Right now, just about everyone is off the yacht and it makes me feel even more vulnerable when it comes to whatever Preston has planned."

"Promise me you're going to be careful."

"I promise, but you have to do the same, and you're not leaving this vessel without your watch and phone. I need to be able to track you, especially if my brother doesn't have anyone here yet."

"It's going to be fine." He cupped her face and kissed her sweet lips. "I'll apologize now for being a jerk."

"Wonderful." She turned and peeked her head out into the hallway. "All clear." She tiptoed around the corner and headed up the staircase.

He waited five minutes before he gathered his watered-down whiskey and opened the door. He sloshed his drink down the front of his salmon-colored shirt. "Fuck. Preston, you scared the shit out of me," he said with his best slow Southern drawl. The one that always came out when he'd had one too many.

"I've got a surprise for you." Preston smacked him on the shoulder. "I'm really surprised how quickly you've come over to my way of thinking."

"I wouldn't say I've done that." Reid stepped out to the back deck by the hot tub and glanced around. Not a single member of the team milled about. No country music echoed from the speakers. The only sounds came from a single engine idling in the water below.

Reid's pulse increased. Perspiration dotted his hairline.

"Not even close. As a matter of fact, all I've done is gotten half-drunk while I tried to figure out how on earth I ended up in this hellhole with you."

"That's not really the attitude that's going to get you out of this mess." Preston waved his hand out in front of the steps that led to the lower deck.

"Nothing can help me at this point."

"You know. You're probably right." Preston reached behind his back and pulled out a handgun.

"What the fuck, Preston?" Reid raised his hands and stumbled down the stairs. "Jesus. Put that fucking thing down."

"No can do." Preston waved it in Reid's face.

Reid swallowed.

Hard.

He'd been around rifles his entire life. As a Texan, it was his birthright, but he didn't like a gun pointed at his face.

Not that he'd ever had that experience before.

He glanced over his shoulder as he inched closer to the water's edge. Falling in might not be a bad idea.

Out of the corner of his eye, the tender came into view. Jim stood behind the center console, both hands gripping the steering wheel. Darcie sat next to him with her hands bound behind her back and tape covering her mouth.

Reid's breath hitched.

"What's going on, Preston?"

"A little change in plans."

"I see that," Reid said. "Mind clueing me in?" He caught Darcie's stoic gaze. His heart squeezed. He couldn't have saved Erin from herself. But he could have prevented this from happening. He should have seen fucking Preston and his games coming from a mile away.

But he hadn't, and now he had to fix things for Darcie.

"Get on the tender." Preston pressed the weapon into the center of Reid's back.

Reid did as instructed, stepping over two sets of scuba diving suits and tanks.

Interesting.

"How are you involved in all of this?" Reid stood in front of Jim and glared.

"Same way you are," Jim said.

"I doubt that." Reid made his way to the other side of the small motorboat. "It would mean you are being blackmailed."

"Maybe I am," Jim said. The right side of his mouth lifted in a snarl. "Your business partner here is a real piece of work."

"Tell me something I don't know," Reid said, kneeling in front of Darcie. "Are you okay?"

She nodded.

"Can I take this off of her? I don't think anyone is going to hear her out here now," Reid said.

"Go ahead." Preston gestured with the gun.

"I'm sorry, but this might hurt." Reid tugged at the corner of the tape, holding the other side tight. "Ready?"

She blinked.

In one quick motion, he yanked.

"Shit. That hurt."

He rubbed his thumb over her lips before giving them a quick kiss. "Sorry. Are you sure you're okay?"

"I'm not dead."

"What a tender moment," Preston said, sitting on the edge of the boat. "Take us to our final destination, Captain Jim."

Jim pressed the throttle and turned the steering wheel, heading north.

Wonderful.

"Are we going for a swim?" Reid rested his hand on Darcie's shoulder, giving her a gentle massage. The boat came around an island and entered a larger body of water. The waves grew bigger as they drove farther away from shore and there wasn't another boat in sight.

Not good.

"Two of you are," Preston said.

Death by scuba accident. Interesting. "Which two, and what's the headline? Because I read my suicide note. This isn't jiving with what you wrote."

Preston jerked his head. "How did you manage to find…? Never mind. It's not important. And you're right. You're not going to die in a scuba diving accident. Darcie and Jim will."

"Excuse me?" Jim pulled back slightly on the throttle. "You're going to do what now?"

"Oh, I'm sorry, Jim. You're no longer useful to me. Did I neglect to inform you of that?" Preston waved his gun. "This is working out better than I planned."

"I don't see how," Jim said.

"It's simple. You and Darcie are going to have a little accident when you go down to get your drugs that you had to hide out here. And, Reid, well…he saw you leave together and was just so out of sorts, he just had to go take that leap off Deception Pass, after all."

"You're not going to get away with this," Reid said.

"Oh. Yes, I am." Preston smiled like a teenage boy who just stole second base.

"I'm curious." Darcie tilted her head at Jim. "How the hell did you and Preston hook up and why? I don't get this partnership."

"It's not a partnership," Jim said. "Never was. I wish I had never met the fucker."

"Feeling is kind of mutual. And perhaps if you

had just done as you were told, we wouldn't be in this situation." Preston rested the gun on his thigh and gripped the console with his free hand as the boat bounced up and down with the waves. "You see, Jim was just supposed to fuck Darcie so when we got on this stupid charter, Reid here would get all jealous and get himself in a drunken stupor. But you had to go and get yourself a little pussy on the side."

"You fucking asshole." Reid launched himself across the boat, shoving Jim to the side.

Preston reached in front of Jim and grabbed Darcie by the hair, yanking her to his chest and shoving the gun against her temple. Preston smiled. "I wouldn't do that if I were you."

"You are a fucking piece of work," Darcie mumbled. "If you think I'm going to let you toss me overboard to drown, you've got another thing coming. I refuse to die that way."

"You refuse." Preston cocked his head. "That's funny. As if you have a choice."

"I'm not going to let you make it look like I died in some random scuba accident digging up drugs with that asshole." She struggled, her hands still bound together at her wrists. "No. You want me dead, then shoot me." She lifted her arms and elbowed him in the gut.

He groaned but didn't budge.

Reid inched closer. He glanced between Jim and Darcie. He didn't trust Jim as far as he could spit, but if what Jim said was true, then he could use Jim's help to get out of this fucking mess. He shifted his gaze to the throttle, then the wheel, hoping Jim wasn't a complete and utter moron.

"Don't tempt me, you fucking bitch." Preston held the gun steady. "Fuck that. I know how to keep you in line. I'll shoot your boyfriend." He changed his aim, pointing the weapon dead center at Reid's chest.

The sound of a deep horn echoed in the dark night. The boat pitched to the right as it rolled over a massive wake wave. Preston grabbed the center console with his free hand.

"Hang onto something." He turned the steering wheel hard to the port side and gunned the engine.

Reid cocked his fist and launched toward Preston. "I hope you fucking rot in hell."

Bang!

Darcie screamed as she fell to the fiberglass floor.

"Fuck." Reid grabbed the right side of his chest. His body flew backward from the velocity of the bullet tearing through his skin and muscles.

Darcie screamed. "Are you okay? Did he shoot you?"

"I'm fine," Reid said, lying through his fucking teeth.

The boat pitched starboard. Preston slammed into the side of the boat. The gun dislodged from his grip and skidded across the bottom of the hull.

Reid struggled through the pain as he crawled across the floor toward the weapon.

Jim kicked at Preston while he maneuvered the boat port and then starboard, zigzagging, heading toward shore.

Darcie struggled to break free of her restraints.

All Reid had to do was get the gun and get the fucking upper hand so they could take this fucker down once and for all.

"Next bullet is going in your heart," Preston said.

"I don't think so." Just as Reid's fingers touched the gun, the boat rolled to the starboard side, pushing the weapon closer to Preston.

Reid let out a long breath as he stared down the wrong end of a handgun. Fuck. Fuck. Fuck.

"I don't think so, you motherfucker." Darcie stood over him with a fire extinguisher. She raised it over her head and swung, bringing it down and across the back of Preston's head. He grunted and fell flat to his stomach. "And you." Darcie picked up the gun and pointed it at Jim. "How fucking dare you? If I thought I could live with myself, I'd pull the trigger."

"That's not a good idea," Reid said between ragged breaths. He clutched his chest and blinked. Everything blurred. He sat down on the back bench. Bile trickled to the back of his throat. "Jim, sit down and put your hands behind your back."

"What?"

"Just fucking do it. Darcie, tie him up. Good."

"Sure thing."

"Seriously? You're going to tie me up after I helped save you? Come on. Can't we just call it even?"

"No. We can't." Reid leaned back on the cold cushion. He kept his focus on Darcie and her movements. He smiled proudly as she handled the rope with ease, securing Jim's hands to the metal posts on the side of the center bench. "And when you're done with him, tie up Preston."

"We don't have cell service right here," Darcie said. "But about two miles closer to the shore, I'll be able to reach the Coast Guard and my brother." She stood at the helm, her hair whipping in the wind. She was the most beautiful thing Reid had ever seen. If he died in this moment, it would be okay because he got to die looking at the woman who mattered the most to him.

"Good. Good," he said. He held his chest, putting as much pressure on the wound as he could. The pain wasn't as horrible as he thought it would be. Not that he thought about what getting shot would be like all that often. Only it burned to breathe, and he couldn't fill his lungs.

"Why don't you call Jagar while I call the Coast Guard?"

He closed his eyes. He told himself it would only be for a minute. He just needed a moment to refresh. Only, he found himself drifting off to dreamland.

"Reid," Darcie said. "Reid?" she repeated.

He opened his mouth, but only gurgling noises came out.

"Oh, my God. You're bleeding. Like really badly."

"Just drive," he said. "Get us to safety. I'll be fine."

"You don't look so well." She pulled her shirt over her head and wadded it up, pressing it over his chest. "You need to come sit next to me. Can you do that?"

"I'll try."

She lifted his arm and looped it over her neck and shoulders.

Leaning the majority of his weight on her, he hobbled toward the center console.

"I'll drive," Jim said.

"You just sit there and be quiet." Darcie eased Reid onto the bench seat. She gripped the steering wheel with one hand and put pressure on his wound with the other. "You should have told me he shot you."

"I should have told you the other day that I love you."

"That, too."

"Do you love me, Darcie?"

"I love you, Reid. With all my heart and soul."

"Good. Good," he whispered. "I want to go to sleep now." He could hear her protesting, but he couldn't fight the darkness anymore. He let it engulf him and accepted it. He'd soon be one with the nothingness, and he'd feel nothing, see nothing, and be nothing.

At the end of the day, it's what they all wanted.

DARCIE PACED in the emergency department waiting room. She'd chewed off three of her nails and had started on a fourth.

"You need to stop. You're making me crazy," Asher said.

Darcie had to admit that Asher had gone above and beyond the call of duty when he showed up at the hospital. He'd only come to town for some conference thing. He hadn't been here for official business, and he and no reason to be hanging out holding her hand.

"Sorry. It's just been four hours since he went into surgery."

"He was shot in the chest, sister." Jagar squeezed her shoulder. "Doctor said it could take a while. The bullet did a fair amount of damage."

"Do you have to remind me that this surgery is life or death?"

Jagar smiled. "The doctor said he would be fine."

"No. The doctor told us that the average person wouldn't have been as coherent as Reid after an injury like that."

"Reid isn't average," her brother said. He had the nerve to remind her of that little piece of information. As if she'd somehow managed to forget that Reid was a bit of perfection.

"Look." Asher took her by the forearms and guided her to the ugly green and brown vinyl chairs that were as hard as a rock. "Jagar and I know doctor speak for gunshot wounds. The worst of Reid's problems, besides being really fucking sore for a while, is a collapsed lung. But that will heal. Trust me. Remember, they didn't start surgery right after they kicked us out of the room. As a matter of fact, for all we know, it could have been an hour before they even opened him up. He could be sitting in recovery right now."

"Here comes Matt," Jagar said. "What did you find out?"

Darcie's heart dropped to the pit of her stomach. "What's Preston saying?" She could only imagine the lies spewing from that man's mouth. Even Jim had started to backpedal when the police finally arrived. While she understood that he didn't want to go to jail, Jim should have thought about that before he went to bed with the likes of Preston.

"He's a fucking whackjob, that's for sure," Matt said. "Delusional would be a grave understatement."

"Please tell me he's not going to get away with this." Darcie brought her hand to the center of her chest. It felt like a baby elephant had just plopped himself down on top of her in preparation for story-time. "If he's come up with some crazy plan that will make all of us look—"

"Darcie. Calm down," Matt said.

She glared at her brother's long-time friend and fellow police officer. "Don't tell me to calm the fuck down. I just had some asshole trying to kill me, and he shot my boyfriend. That pisses me off."

"Then this should make you feel better." Matt squeezed her shoulder. "Jim cracked under pressure and confessed to running drugs."

"Preston had him running drugs? Why?" Asher asked.

"No. Jim was doing that on his own. That's what Preston had on Jim, and he was using it to blackmail him," Matt said. "Preston is a sick motherfucker. He said all he wanted to do was watch Reid fall apart when he saw you and Jim together. And then, of course, kill Reid, making it look like a suicide. When Jim got caught cheating, Preston had to change his plans. But the bottom line had always been to kill Reid and make it look like he offed himself, which in turn would leave the company to Preston outright. But instead, Preston is going to find out what it's like to live in a nine-by-six cell for the next twenty years."

"Thank God." She shook out her hands, focused her gaze back on the floor, and paced in front of the ugly metal chairs.

"A man like Preston won't do well in prison," Asher said.

"I really don't care." Darcie rubbed the back of her neck. "What about Jim? What's going to happen to him?"

"He could potentially avoid jail time because he's a small piece of a very large drug trafficking ring involving superyachts. If Jim is smart, he'll cut a deal," Matt said. "Looks like we get to hear about our boy." Matt pointed to the doctor stepping through the automatic doors.

Darcie shoved Asher and Matt to the side. She took her brother's hand and squeezed it hard. "Hey, doc, how is he?" Her vocal cords trembled. She pinched her thigh.

"He's asking to be discharged, so I'd say he's doing quite well," the doctor said. "The surgery went fine. We patched up his lung and removed the bullet. He'll need oxygen for a day or two, so we'll keep him for at least another twenty-four hours. He's got a cracked rib, but other than that, he'll be as good as new in a few weeks."

Jagar looped his arm around her shoulders. "See? He's going to be just fine."

"I'll believe that when I see him."

"That can be arranged. Though only one at a time," the doctor said.

"Obviously, I'm the one going in." She gave her brother a big hug. "Thanks for having my back."

"Always. And for the record, I heard you were pretty amazing out there."

"I was." She smiled. "I'm not leaving this hospital, so go ahead and go home. I'll call you later."

Jagar kissed her cheek.

"Hey, Asher. I'm sorry. But I don't think I'll be able to take you and the family sailing on Sunday."

Asher pulled her in for a warm hug. "No worries. Tell Reid I better not have to ever punch him again."

Oh, boy. She had no idea if she and Reid even stood a chance. There was so much to discuss, and she had one very major decision to make about her career. As much as she loved Reid, it still seemed doomed.

She strolled down the long corridor, glancing at the names on the outside of the doors. Nurses and doctors and other visitors huddled in various corners, all in deep conversations. When she found Reid's room, she gripped the curtain, held it for a long moment, and then took in a deep breath. She plastered on a smile and pulled back the fabric.

Reid lay on the bed, raised slightly. A thin sheet covered his body to his waist. Bandages were wrapped around his middle. He blinked open his eyes. "There you are," he said, licking his lips. "Can you hand me that water?" He raised his finger slightly. It shook.

"Sure." She brought the straw to his mouth and held his gaze. She ran her hand over his forehead.

"You are a sight for sore eyes."

She leaned over and pressed her lips to his temple. "If you ever get hurt again and not tell me, I'll shoot you myself."

"Since I never want to experience that again, I'll make sure not to keep that from you."

Sitting on the edge of the bed, she held his hand, running her fingers up and down his arm. "I've never been so scared before in my life."

"You know what scares me?"

"No. What?"

"Spending another day without you in my life. I love you."

"I love you, too." She let out a long breath.

"We have a lot of things to work out."

"We sure do."

"I want you to know I won't ask you to give up your job this time. I might follow you around more after I get this shit figured out with my company."

She blinked out a tear.

He groaned as he reached up and cupped her cheek. "What's the matter?"

"Our worlds are so far apart."

"So, we bring them together. Hell. I'll move to Seattle and live on your sailboat if you want."

"You'd do that just to be with me?"

"I lost you once because I was an idiot." He smoothed down her hair. "I'm not about to do that again. It's going to take some work on our part to figure out the logistics, but we'll do it. And this time, we don't have people in our lives manipulating us."

She smiled. "No. We have family supporting us."

"I like the sound of that."

"You know what I'd really like?"

"Tell me."

"I'd like for us to take some time off and maybe sail down to that island you live on in Galveston. Will you sail with me?"

"I'll go anywhere with you."

EPILOGUE

Two weeks later…

*R*eid stepped out onto the deck and set his mug down on the table. He slowly raised his arms to the sky and stretched. He groaned. It still hurt like a motherfucker. And taking in a full deep breath still hadn't become possible.

One thing was for sure, though, he could get used to living on a sailboat.

It really was like *Living the Dream.*

He glanced toward the bright blue sky. Not a cloud in sight.

Quietly, he closed the door to the galley and made himself comfortable on the stern in what had become his favorite spot. He flicked open the paper and scanned the headlines.

He was getting really tired of reading about himself and Preston. It would die down eventually.

However, it might get worse before it got better, especially since he'd uncovered that Preston had started cutting corners in areas that could have cost lives. Reid would have to make some serious adjustments to his business, one of which would be to sell off a few divisions.

Enough was enough.

Reid really wanted to focus on a few things and do them right. His company had gotten too big and spread out. It was time to bring it back to the basics. Besides, he really wanted to spend every waking moment with Darcie when she was around, and thank God her season had wrapped up last night. She had a full six weeks off before she captained her first full season on a superyacht out of Key West. He was looking forward to it since he planned to relocate to south Florida for the duration of the charter season.

Their life would be like that for two years, and then Darcie said she wanted to open a sailing school.

The only question was whether it would be in Galveston or Seattle.

Thud.

Bang.

Crash.

Thud.

What the fuck?

Reid leaped from his chair. He groaned, clutching his side as he fumbled down the five steps into the galley where he saw Darcie's feet sticking out of the bathroom. "What's wrong?"

She answered with a noise that he would have preferred not to hear. She coughed and gagged.

Holding back her hair, he rubbed her back. "I guess we're not going to the market this morning."

"No. We can still go." She brushed the hair from her face and took the hand he offered. "Get me a glass of juice and some crackers, please."

"Sure thing." He helped her to the sofa, brushing his lips over her forehead. "You don't feel warm."

"I'm not sick."

"I beg to differ, considering what I just witnessed."

"I knew I should have told you this last night." She took the juice he offered and sucked down half of it.

"Now you're freaking me out."

"You might want to sit down for this." She brought a cracker to her plump lips and nibbled.

He let out a short breath and joined her on the

sofa. "I'm listening." He ran a hand through his hair, doing his best to push all negative thoughts away. They'd made a lot of decisions, and while that made him ridiculously happy, there was still a tiny little voice in the back of his head that warned him this wasn't going to be smooth sailing.

"Do you remember when we first got together, and we didn't use a condom, and you said there wasn't anything we could do about it and we'd just have to wait and see?"

His mind got stuck on *didn't use a condom.* He replayed the words over and over again. He remembered the encounter like it was yesterday, and he also recalled being concerned for about five seconds that she could be pregnant. But he hadn't given it another thought since that moment.

"Well, the waiting is over." She waved the cracker. "Not only are you an extremest, but it looks like your sperm are, too."

"Are you sure? How can you be sure?"

"I peed on a stick yesterday morning while on charter. I brought another one home to double-check. But this is the fourth morning in a row I've gotten sick."

"I guess morning sex is out of the question." He swallowed. "A baby?"

She set the box of crackers on the coffee table.

She straddled his legs and cupped his face. "I know this wasn't part of the two-year plan."

"Nope. It wasn't." He gripped her hips. "I can't believe it."

"Me either." She lowered her forehead to his. "This is a big deal. Are you okay with it? It's going to change everything for us. All the things we thought we could put off deciding for a year or so, we're going to have to figure out now."

He splayed his hands across her back. "I'm totally on board with us having a baby, but I don't see the urgency."

She opened her mouth, but he hushed it with a quick kiss.

"Seriously. We're going to have to pick a city. I'm going to need to put in my resignation and—"

"You will do no such thing." He tapped her nose. "If you want to do a few charters while you're pregnant and the doctor says it's okay, then it's fine with me. You can even do some after. I'm sure I can handle being a full-time dad."

"I don't know about after I have this kid, but I would at least like to do the two seasons while I'm pregnant." She tilted her head and smiled. "Are we actually talking like we're both very okay with having a family?"

"I think we are." His heart swelled and tears

burned the corners of his eyes. He'd spent his entire life chasing thrills.

But nothing could have prepared him for the adrenaline rush scorching through his system right now after finding out that he was about to be a parent.

It was truly the sensation he'd been searching for since he could remember.

"However, we can't raise a baby on this boat," he said. "And while I do have a big beautiful place in Texas, there's no family there. Most of your family is here in Seattle. We should move here."

"I'm not selling my boat."

"I didn't ask you to." He laughed. "You know what we should do this weekend?" He jumped to his feet, setting her gently on the sofa. He knelt in front of her. "I'm not doing this right at all, but it's not like we've been conventional about anything."

"What are you babbling about?"

"Let's get married."

Her jaw dropped open. "Seriously?"

"Why not? And don't tell me you want a church wedding with the white dress because I know you, Darcie Bowie. That's the last thing you'd want."

"You're right about that."

"We can get married right here and then sail off

to our honeymoon. What do you say? Will you sail with me?"

She took his chin with her thumb and forefinger. "You don't even really know how to sail."

"So, teach me."

"I love you, Reid."

"Let's live the dream. Together."

THE END

THE WITH ME IN SEATTLE UNIVERSE

For More information about The With Me in Seattle Universe, click here:

https://www.ladybosspress.com/with-me-in-seattle

DESTINY'S DREAM

Federal Investigators
JANE DOE'S RETURN
THE BUTTERFLY MURDERS

The Aegis Network
THE LIGHTHOUSE
HER LAST HOPE
THE LAST FLIGHT
THE RETURN HOME
THE MATRIARCH

The Collective Order
THE LOST SISTER
THE LOST SOLDIER
THE LOST SOUL
THE LOST CONNECTION
A Spin-Off Series: Witches Academy Series
THE NEW ORDER

Special Forces Operation Alpha
BURNING DESIRE
BURNING KISS

BURNING SKIES

BURNING LIES

BURNING HEART

BURNING BED

REMEMBER ME ALWAYS

The Brotherhood Protectors

Out of the Wild

ROUGH JUSTICE

ROUGH AROUND THE EDGES

ROUGH RIDE

ROUGH EDGE

ROUGH BEAUTY

The Brotherhood Protectors

The Saving Series

SAVING LOVE

SAVING MAGNOLIA

Holiday Romances

A CHRISTMAS GETAWAY

ALASKAN CHRISTMAS

WHISPERS

Heroes & Heroines on the Field

TAKING A RISK

TEE TIME

The Twilight Crossing Series

THE BLIND DATE

SPRING FLING

SUMMER'S GONE

WINTER WEDDING

Witches and Werewolves

LADY SASS

ALL THAT SASS

ABOUT JEN TALTY

Welcome to my World! I'm a USA Today Bestseller of Romantic Suspense, Contemporary Romance, and Paranormal Romance.

I first started writing while carting my kids to one hockey rink after the other, averaging 170 games per year between 3 kids in 2 countries and 5 states. My first book, IN TWO WEEKS was originally published in 2007. In 2010 I helped form a publishing company (Cool Gus Publishing) with NY Times Bestselling Author Bob Mayer where I ran the technical side of the business through 2016.

I'm currently enjoying the next phase of my life...the empty NESTER! My husband and I spend our winters in Jupiter, Florida and our summers in Rochester, NY. We have three amazing children who have all gone off to carve out their places in the world, while I continue to craft stories that I hope will make you readers feel good and put a smile on your face.

Sign up for my Newsletter (https://dl.bookfunnel.com/6atcf7g1be) where I often give away free books before publication.

Join my private Facebook group (https://www.facebook.com/groups/191706547909047/) where I post exclusive excerpts and discuss all things murder and love!

Never miss a new release. Follow me on Amazon:amazon.com/author/jentalty

And on Bookbub: bookbub.com/authors/jentalty

Made in the USA
Coppell, TX
06 December 2020

42922298R00163